While out on an assignment for the Shifter Council, Enforcer Dane Drudeson runs across his mate—the human Danny Nunez. He could have called in a replacement and stuck close to the man to woo him, but due to the time-sensitive nature of his mission, he chooses not to. Instead, Dane seduces the sweet, sexy human and secures his phone number. Knowing where Danny works and the town he lives in, Dane feels confident he can track Danny down when he comes back in a few days. Except, after Dane secures time off and returns to the small town, Danny is gone, forcing Dane to go on the hunt. After discovering Danny was injured by his own father, then driven out of town by bigotry, can Dane track down the other half of his soul before something else happens to his sweet, vulnerable human?

Hunting his Human
Copyright © 2021 Charlie Richards
ISBN: 978-1-4874-3459-5
Cover art by Angela Waters

Published by eXtasy Books Inc

Look for us online at:
www.eXtasybooks.com

Hunting his Human
Shifter's Regime Book Nine

By

Charlie Richards

DEDICATION

I don't think it's about finding who you are. I think it's about finding a place where you can be who you are.
~Unknown

CHAPTER ONE

Daniel Nunez — but everyone called him Danny — watched the pair of men join an already seated couple in his section of the diner. They greeted each other with smiles and handshakes, then settled at the table. All four of the men were good-looking, but the new guy with the shaggy blond hair caused Danny's heart to race and his blood to flow south.

He was *that* good-looking.

Not that Danny would ever hit on a customer, but he would certainly enjoy dreaming about him while jacking off in the shower after his shift. Besides, the big blond was most likely straight, and no way did Danny want a customer to complain about his behavior. He needed his job too much.

With his order pad in hand, Danny headed toward the table. At least one look in Peggy's direction — the woman working as a hostess that day — caused his plumping dick to wilt. From day one, that woman hadn't liked him. Danny didn't know how she knew he was gay, but she'd made her view of him clear swiftly enough — just never within earshot of anyone else.

Danny wished he could find other employment, but jobs were scarce in his podunk little town.

Someday, things will be different. Someday, I'll get out of here. Just not today.

Stopping beside the table, Danny heard the sexy blond rumble, "Naw. Don't worry about it," as he waved his hand as if shooing away a fly.

The deep timbre caused a fresh spike of lust to shoot

1

through Danny, and he had to swallow swiftly in order to keep from drooling.

Then . . . the man turned his attention on Danny, and he felt himself get caught by the warm, brown-eyed gaze that threatened to make him swoon.

"Hello, cutie," the man greeted, confidence filling his tone. "How about a cup of coffee? And how are your pancakes?"

Holy crapballs. Did he just call me cute?

Right. Pancakes. Work.

Finding his tongue, Danny stuttered, "O-Our pancakes are e-excellent, sir." He would forever deny the slight squeak in his voice. Scrambling to find something normal to say, Danny added, "As are the sausage links."

Oh, shit. Why did I have to mention sausage?

The guy grinned broadly as he glanced at his friends. "We're not in a hurry, are we?"

The dark-haired man who'd entered with him replied, "Nope. Take your time, Dane. We got all morning."

Dane. What a sexy name. Danny and Dane.

Danny's brain supplied an image of a heart with D plus D etched into a tree.

Good grief. Stop thinking like a teenage girl.

"Excellent." Dane returned his focus to Danny, and he finally understood the term eye-fucking. His blood rushed through his veins, and his face heated. Danny knew he was blushing, but he couldn't have stopped it if he'd tried.

When Dane continued speaking, Danny did his best to focus, but boy, was it difficult.

"I'll take your farmer's platter and upgrade that to all-you-can-eat pancakes."

Jotting that down on his order pad, Danny asked, "A-And how would you like your eggs?" Danny couldn't help the way his voice sounded a little rough. The sexy man was just that amazing.

"Over-easy," Dane replied, glancing at his nametag before

meeting his gaze again. "Danny."

Hearing Dane say his name in his sexy rumbly voice caused a tremor to work through him. Danny hoped no one saw.

"A-And to d-drink?" Speaking wasn't getting any easier, but Danny tried to focus on his job. If Peggy was watching, he couldn't be seen flirting.

As if I know how to flirt.

"Coffee," Dane replied. "Danny."

Crap. He said that already.

Turning, Danny took a couple of steps, needing to get away from the sexy man. He groaned in his mind as he recalled that there were others sitting at the table. Focusing on his order pad, he returned to the table and asked after the other men's needs, although he couldn't manage to make himself meet their gazes.

Danny hurried to the kitchen to place their orders and get their drinks. The hairs on his nape prickled, and he just knew if he peeked back at the table, Danny would see Dane watching him with his warm, intense gaze. Unfortunately, a glance out of the corner of Danny's eyes told him that Peggy was watching, too.

After clipping the order to the board, Danny quickly whipped up a fresh hot chocolate. He placed that on a tray along with several mugs and a small plate holding a fresh pot of hot water and a new tea bag. Carrying that in one hand, Danny grabbed the coffee pot as he passed it.

Girding up his courage, Danny returned to the table containing the sexy Dane and his friends. He quickly gave everyone their drinks, earning thanks from everyone except the dreamboat. Unable to help himself, Danny glanced furtively at the man in question.

Dane smiled and winked at him. Then he glanced meaningfully at a napkin as he slid it toward Danny.

After a second of hesitation, Danny tucked the tray under

the arm holding the coffee pot and grabbed the folded napkin. He shoved it into his pocket before heading away, returning the tray to his now free hand. His heart beat wildly as he stopped at a table to top off another customer's cup of coffee. Danny checked on other tables as he passed, but no one needed anything.

After returning the coffee pot to the warmer and putting the tray where it belonged, Danny glanced about. With no one paying him any mind, he pulled the napkin from his pocket. Danny couldn't do anything about his shaking hands as he unfolded it.

Upon reading the message written in a bold, blocky script, Danny's breath caught in his throat.

Meet me in the men's room so I can get your phone number and a kiss.

Oh, shit. Wow!

Danny's heart pounded in his chest, and butterflies seemed to have taken up residence in his belly.

Am I really about to get my first kiss? Do I want to?

From Dane? Hell, yeah.

Peering around the opening that led to the diner's seating area, Danny sought out Peggy and the others on duty. Gloria was smiling and chatting with a table in her section while Donna was in the kitchen plating up someone's order. To Danny's surprise, one of Dane's buddies stood next to Peggy, and whatever they were talking about clearly had the hostess entranced.

Danny looked toward Dane's table just in time to see the man in question heading toward the men's room.

Knowing it was now or never, Danny headed back into the kitchen. "Hey, Clark," he called, addressing one of the line cooks. "I'll be back in a sec. Gonna hit the head."

Clark nodded, not bothering to look up from the salad he

was working on. "Don't forget to wash your hands."

Danny forced a chuckle around his nerves. "I won't."

Then Danny headed to the men's room. He paused for a second outside the door, taking a deep breath for strength. After letting it out, he headed inside.

The restaurant's men's room was standard for a diner. There were two stalls, two urinals, and two sinks. Danny spotted Dane leaning against the counter containing the sinks and froze.

Dane seemed so much taller and broader while standing up—and so much sexier. His blue jeans appeared almost painted on, showcasing long legs and thick muscles. His polo shirt was much the same, the deep green looking magnificent on his olive-tanned skin. With one ankle crossed over the other, one hip leaning against the ugly blue counter, Dane looked like the epitome of masculinity.

Danny couldn't imagine why the powerful-looking man seemed interested in him.

"Thank you for coming, Danny," Dane rumbled in his deep, sexy voice.

Dragging his gaze to Dane's face, Danny saw the heat in his eyes. "Um, s-sure."

"I know we don't have much time," Dane continued, pushing away from the counter. Slowly, he stalked toward him with predatory grace. "But my friend will keep Peggy occupied for a few minutes, anyway."

As Dane grew closer, Danny tipped his head back . . . and back, in order to hold his gaze.

Oh, wow. He's tall!

"Y-You want my ph-phone number?" Danny whispered.

"Very much so," Dane told him, boldly reaching for him . . . and past him. After flipping the lock on the bathroom door, he placed one hand on Danny's hip and cupped his jaw with the other. "As well as a kiss." His eyes appeared to be warm chocolate pools as he began to dip his head. "May I,

Danny?"

Danny's flesh heated where Dane touched him, and goose bumps erupted on his neck and arms.

Dane's face stopped a hairsbreadth from his own. The man's eyes were heavy-lidded, and Danny couldn't tear his gaze away. His pulse pounded in anticipation.

"Danny?" Dane rumbled.

"Y-Yes," Danny whispered, his voice coming out huskier than he'd ever heard it before.

A deep groan erupted from Dane. Then his lips were on Danny's. On instinct, Danny gripped Dane's shirt and closed his eyes as Dane's flesh moved against his own.

Dane teased lightly, eased away, then returned. It felt as if Dane was learning him, and Danny trembled as heat erupted in his gut. Feeling Dane's tongue swipe along his bottom lip, Danny opened.

With a low groan, Dane accepted Danny's invitation, thrusting his tongue into his mouth. He tightened his hand on Danny's face while sliding his arm around his waist. Pulling Danny close, Dane tilted their heads, sealing their mouths more fully.

Danny's cock throbbed behind his fly as he reveled in the taste of the other man. There was the obvious flavor of coffee, but underneath that, there was something masculine that had to be all Dane. Danny shuddered as he pressed closer, wanting more.

Dane growled into his mouth, sweeping his tongue deep. His arm around his waist tightened even further as he released Danny's face. That hand landed on Danny's ass, and he found himself lifted and spun.

On instinct, Danny wrapped his legs around the huge man's waist. He whimpered when his cock was pressed against something equally hard . . . and much larger. Unable to help himself, Danny bucked in Dane's hold, giving in to his need for pressure.

Suddenly, Dane lifted his head, ending the kiss. "Fucking hell," he snarled.

Danny felt the counter under his ass and snapped his eyes open. The other man's tone worried him, but only for an instant. Then he met Dane's gaze and saw the feral lust darkening his chocolate eyes almost to black.

"I was just going to kiss you," Dane rumbled, his chest heaving just as much as Danny's. "But, gods, the way you respond."

When Dane cupped his erection through his jeans, Danny gasped and rocked into his hold.

"Yeah," Dane muttered, a hungry grin curving his lips. "Need to touch."

Dane didn't ask permission as he had with the kiss. He had Danny's fly opened, his underwear pushed down, and Danny's dick in his hand with shocking speed. Danny bit his bottom lip and bucked, only Dane's big body keeping him from rocking right off the counter.

Danny had never felt anything as amazing as Dane's huge hand on the sensitive skin of his shaft. His eyes gleamed with something unreadable as he jacked him. The pleasure went straight to his balls, and Danny knew he was going to blow in seconds.

Just when Danny feared he was about to make a mess out of his work clothes, Dane dropped to his knees and swallowed his cock to the root. Wet heat caused his brain to fuzz out. He arched, his head tipping back on a silent scream — thankfully — as his orgasm barreled through him. Wave upon wave of heady bliss sizzled across his nerve endings, and Dane kept sucking, drinking his seed, causing the sensations to go on and on.

Finally, when the stimulation became too much, Danny whimpered. Dane immediately popped off his dick. He didn't stand, instead, resting his cheek on Danny's thigh. Panting, he peered up at Danny, a satisfied-looking smile curving his full lips.

Unable to believe what had just happened—in his work's bathroom, no less—Danny just stared.

"You are delicious, my mate," Dane murmured before sighing deeply. Slowly, he stood before resting his hands on Danny's hips. "Can't wait to do that again." Dane winked. "In a bed, next time."

Holy shit. He wants a next time?

Tearing his focus away from Dane's pleased smile, Danny realized something else. Dane's fly was open, and his half-hard dick was on clear display. Danny gulped at the sight of the huge cock the other guy sported, although, considering the man's massive size, it made sense.

That didn't stop the nerves from firing through his system for a whole new reason.

Does he expect me to be able to take that?

"Hey, easy, Danny," Dane crooned, rubbing his big palms up and down Danny's sides soothingly. "Don't worry. You'll be well-prepared, honey." With crooked forefingers under Danny's chin, Dane urged him to meet his gaze. "I would never hurt you. I promise."

So, yeah. He must want more.

Gulping, Danny murmured, "Um, okay." Knowing he needed to be honest with the big man, he admitted, "I've just, um, I've never—" Danny felt his cheeks heat once more as embarrassment swamped him.

Dane's eyes narrowed as a low growl rumbled from him. "Oh, Danny. What a gift you are." He dipped his head and pressed a hard kiss to Danny's lips before taking a step back and doing up his pants. "Come on."

After helping Danny off the counter, Dane tucked him away, which pulled a gasp from him as his gut clenched. His sensitive dick even tried to rise once more. Dane just smiled as he finished, then returned his hand to cradle Danny's jaw.

"I would apologize for mauling you, my mate, but you tasted so damn sweet," Dane told him with a wry grin and a shrug of his massive shoulders. "Plus, it would be a lie, since I enjoyed every second of it." Still smiling, he added, "So" — he pulled out his phone with his free hand — "your phone number?"

Danny rattled off the number, all the while wondering if Dane would actually call.

"And what time do you get off your shift?" Dane asked, shoving his phone back into his pocket. "That way, I know when it's safe to call."

"I'm off at three this afternoon," Danny told him, hope flaring within him. "After the lunch rush is over."

Dane nodded. "Okay." Dipping his head once more, he pressed a light peck to his lips. "You can head out first. I'll clean up the mess I made all over the floor," he added with a wink.

Glancing down, Danny realized there were streaks of cum underneath the sinks, and his face flared hot again as the truth finally settled into his addled brain.

Holy camolies. I just made it with some guy I don't know in my work bathroom.

If anyone found out, Danny knew he would be fired in an instant.

"Don't worry," Dane assured, somehow catching onto his thoughts. "No one came round. I'd have heard them, if they did." Massaging Danny's shoulder, Dane told him, "Your secret is safe with me."

Because he could do nothing else, he nodded.

"Probably head to the break room first, honey," Dane urged, teasing his thumb under his jaw. "Straighten yourself up just a little."

Nodding again, Danny started toward the door. Just before he unlocked it, Dane gripped his wrist and turned him around once more. The huge man kissed him hard, then released him and stepped backward.

"Talk to you soon, Danny." Then Dane's brows furrowed. "What's your last name?"

Snickering under his breath, Danny murmured, "Nunez." He peered at Dane through his lashes. "And you?"

Dane grinned broadly. "Drudeson." Tapping his chest, he winked. "Dane Drudeson, and I'll be seeing you again soon."

With his heart still pounding in his chest, Danny unlocked the bathroom, glanced around quickly, and headed to the breakroom.

He had no idea how he managed to finish his shift.

CHAPTER TWO

Walking away from his Fate-given mate was the hardest thing Dane Drudeson had ever done, even knowing it was temporary. He'd constantly reminded the snarling komodo dragon that he shared his psyche with that it wouldn't be for long. Unfortunately, completing the mission that had him in the middle of rural Pennsylvania had taken longer than the single morning he'd planned.

Dane had been in the area to escort a giraffe shifter—Kavan—onto his ex-herd's grounds in order to see his parents. He'd also been ordered to investigate why the herd's alpha—Anthony—hadn't reported it when Kavan had ended up missing. The answer had been simple enough. Anthony was a bigoted bastard. As it had turned out, so were most of the rest of the herd's inner circle. When Kavan's mate—a demon by the name of Beltine—had demanded restitution since Anthony's actions had caused Kavan to be held by a circle of witches for around a decade, Anthony and most of his inner circle had attacked them.

There did end up being one good giraffe in the bunch—Enforcer Godfrey. The shifter had refused to attack them, realizing his alpha's folly. Dane had promoted Godfrey to the alpha position.

Then they'd had to wait for more Shifter Council enforcers to arrive in order to take the alpha, the beta, and the other two enforcers back to headquarters in Georgia. Plus, they'd had to make certain the pack accepted Godfrey as alpha, which they had. Evidently, Anthony had been an asshole to more than just gay shifters, but he had been the strongest of them, and no one had the ability to challenge him for the position. The herd-members were very happy about the change.

All's well that ends well.

Now, I just need to get back to my mate.

Dane had spoken with Danny on the phone every evening, and they texted back and forth quite a bit. With his mate being human, he knew he had to woo his sweet little man. He really had only intended to share a few kisses in the bathroom and get his phone number. Dane hadn't anticipated the strength of the pull he would feel once he had Danny alone.

But, gods, had it been delicious.

The first time Dane had called Danny, on the evening they'd met, he'd heard the surprise in Danny's voice when he'd answered. He knew his mate hadn't believed that he would actually call. Dane figured he thought it was a one-off, but he quickly dispelled that notion.

And now, it's time for me to get back there.

The average human didn't know about paranormals, and for good reason. He would need to woo his mate. While their chemistry was off the charts, he knew he would need to win his human's heart, too. His plan was to do that before explaining that he was a shifter—a creature that shared his psyche with a fucking big komodo dragon and could change into the animal at will.

Smiling as he strode through the Shifter Council headquarters, Dane hurried to Councilman Regales Colearian's offices. He knew the councilman would be finishing up for the day, and he needed to catch him before the bear shifter returned home to his own mate, Theo. As a Council Enforcer, Dane couldn't just disappear, and he knew his longtime friend would be happy to grant him leave.

The councilman would pass on the information to head enforcer, Mycroft—who'd already congratulated him—but Dane needed a councilman's permission, too.

After knocking on the door and hearing Regales's shout for him to enter, Dane did just that. He spotted his friend just where he thought he would be, in the process of closing his laptop and rising to his feet. Dane also noticed Enforcer Igor — a massive wolf shifter — stood off to one side acting as Regales's protection detail for the day.

Dane dipped his head in a nod to Igor. "I'll walk the councilman out, if that's okay with you, Enforcer Igor." He smiled as he saw Igor tip his head to the side inquisitively, reminiscent of the wolf he shared his psyche with. "I need to talk to him anyway."

Igor turned his attention to Regales. "Is that acceptable, Councilman Colearian?"

Regales picked up his suit jacket and slung it over his shoulder rather than don it. "As long as whatever you're going to say doesn't keep me here at the office," he warned with a mock scowl.

Shaking his head, Dane grinned at Regales. "No, sir. It won't." Well, not for longer than it would take to shoot off a message on his phone.

"It's fine, Enforcer Igor." Regales's features eased into a relaxed smile. "You can head out."

Igor dipped his chin in a nod before heading toward the door. "Good evening then, Councilman Colearian. Enforcer Dane." Then the Russian-born wolf shifter headed out of the office.

Shoving his hand into his pocket, Regales pulled out a ring of keys. "So, what's up, Dane?" Regales asked, dropping any formality with just the two of them there.

Grinning at the grizzly shifter, Dane claimed, "I met my mate."

Regales's dark brows shot up even as a broad smile creased his features. "Really? That's fantastic?" He started toward the door. "Where? When? Who?"

Dane preceded Regales out of the office as he chuckled. Glancing up and down the hall, he answered as Regales locked his office door. Due to still being in the process of clearing out some riff-raff who were in the building, Dane knew it was a good precaution.

"On the mission I just finished," Dane told him, continuing to grin broadly as pride surged through him. He'd been so damn jealous when his elder brother, Delanrue, had stumbled upon his mate—not that he would ever share that with the man. *And now, I've found my own.* "A human waiter at the diner where I met Kavan and Beltine. I need a councilman to sign off on the leave paperwork I filed with Mycroft."

"Of course. I'd be happy to," Regales replied, sounding happy for him. He shoved his keys into his pocket and pulled out his phone as he started walking down the hall. "I'll do it right now."

Dane continued to grin as he walked with Regales. "I appreciate that. Thanks, Reg."

Regales nodded absently, his focus remaining on his phone for a moment. They stopped at the elevator, and Dane pushed the button for them. As they stepped into the car, Regales tapped his screen one last time before lowering it.

"Done," Regales declared. Smiling at Dane, he added, "So, a human. Male, I assume, since you said waiter?" As Dane nodded, Regales sobered, "I'm surprised you left him."

Shrugging, Dane admitted, "It was damn tough, but I didn't want to come off like an overbearing asshole." He shoved his hands into his jeans pockets and told him, "So, I got his phone number, and we've been talking and texting. I told him I travel a lot for my job, which is true, but I planned to be back his way in a few days, and I wanted to take him on a date." Meeting Regales's understanding gaze, Dane shared, "He's living in this podunk town in Pennsylvania that's not gay-friendly at all. He still lives with his father even though he's twenty-two, and I'm trying to figure out that dynamic, but he changes the subject every time I bring it up." Rubbing the back of his neck in agitation, Dane finished, "And I have no clue how to explain paranormals and shifters to him. How do I even start *that* conversation?"

Having exited the elevator on the main floor, Regales patted him on the shoulder. "You know Fate doesn't make mistakes. You'll find a way, my friend."

They walked into the parking garage, and Dane swept his gaze around the area, confirming the councilman's safety. Then they headed to his SUV.

"I figure I'll earn his trust first and kinda feel my way along."

"If you need help, call Seever or Tideus. They both mated humans," Regales reminded him. "They may be able to give you pointers."

Dane nodded thoughtfully. "Yeah."

Seever Kerns was a lion shifter in Councilman Vincentius's employ. His human, Reese Nelson, had visited the estate to see his cousin, who'd been living there, and Seever had been overjoyed to discover they were mates. Dane knew Reese's cousin had already known about shifters, having been mated to one, so perhaps either couple could give him some pointers.

Tideus was another good option. A fellow council enforcer, the massive saltwater crocodile shifter had had a bit of a tough go first thing. His newly discovered mate, Sin, had been accused of working with rogues. Sin had been cleared, but what a way to get introduced to paranormals, having been hauled in by Tideus himself for questioning.

"How'd your brothers take it?" Regales asked as he unlocked his SUV, the machine chirping softly. "Do I need to issue them leaves of absences, too?"

"Oh, fuck," Dane muttered, grimacing.

Regales tipped his head back and laughed, the booming sound echoing through the space. "You didn't tell them, yet?"

Shaking his head, Dane admitted, "I was just so focused on completing everything I needed to get done so I could get back there." Dane smiled sheepishly. "I haven't even seen them."

"Well, if they end up needing leaves of absences, tell them to message me." Regales patted Dane on the shoulder as he continued to grin at him. "Good luck, my friend."

Dane nodded. "Thank you. I'm heading out right now." Dane indicated his *Harley Electra Road Glide* parked three spaces down. "I can't wait to feel his arms wrapped around me on my bike."

Regales smiled and nodded. "Drive safely." Then he climbed into his vehicle.

Leaving him to it, Dane crossed to his own ride. He heard Regales's SUV fire up as he pulled his leather chaps from a saddlebag. After donning them, he pulled on his leather jacket. Finally, Dane grabbed his helmet, which had been hanging on a handlebar. He knew he had matching gear in the back bag, and he was pretty certain it would fit his mate.

I can hardly wait.

Dane swung aboard his *Road Glide* and fired it up. The gentle vibration stimulated his balls, and he grinned as his prick swiftly rose to half-mast. Of course, that could have been from the fact that he was thinking about his mate, too.

As Dane left the parking garage, he was aware the standard drive would take approximately eleven hours. With the way his dragon was riding him, he knew he would be shaving off some of that time. He hoped by driving all night, he could be at the diner upon opening, allowing him to see his mate first thing in the morning.

Anticipation caused his gut to clench as he revved his engine and started on his way.

Dane was only an hour into the drive when the *Bluetooth* in his helmet notified him that he had an incoming call. Tapping his phone, which was clipped into the holder to his left, he saw it was Dakota, his younger brother. Unable to help himself, he grinned as he answered the call.

"Hey, Dakota. What's up, man?"

"I can hear that you're on your bike," Dakota replied by way of greeting. "Does that mean you're on your way here?"

"On my way?" Confusion filled Dane. "Uh, no. Why?"

"Damn it, Dane." Dakota sounded thoroughly disgruntled. "You forgot, didn't you?"

Dane obviously had. "Uh, guess so." There was no point in denying it.

Dakota's long-suffering sigh sounded through the line. "It's Miggs's birthday party."

Sucking in a sharp breath, Dane hissed, "Oh, fuck."

Miggs was Delanrue's guinea pig shifter mate. His brother was going to fucking kill him. Except, even as regret turned his stomach, he refused to turn around.

"I need you to make my regrets to them, Dakota," Dane replied in a serious tone. "Something important has come up."

"I heard you were meeting with Regales."

How Dakota knew that, Dane had no idea. The man seemed to always be on top of shifter gossip.

"That's right," Dane confirmed.

"Were you sent out on assignment?" Dakota pressed.

"No, but I am heading back to Pennsylvania. I—"

"If you're not on assignment, why the hell would you head north instead of coming here?" his brother cut in, annoyance and confusion clear in his voice.

"I met my mate up there," Dane told him, excitement filling him anew at being able to claim that.

Dane counted in his head. *One heartbeat. Two.*

"You met your mate?" Dakota cried, all annoyance gone to

be replaced by joy. "Well, fucking hell, man. Congratulations." Then he asked, "If your mate's a giraffe shifter, how come you didn't bring him or her home with you yesterday?"

Realizing Dakota had gotten the wrong idea—that Dane's mate was part of Kavan's old herd—he chuckled. "Not a giraffe, Dakota. My mate is human. He was my waiter at the diner." Just thinking about the slender, sexy human with the short, light-brown hair and gorgeous hazel eyes caused his heart to beat faster and his cock to thicken. "I have to get back to him."

"Okay, I can understand that," Dakota conceded. "I'll pass on your regrets to Del and Miggs. They'll totally understand." After a few seconds, Dakota added, "Let us know if you need anything. We'll back you up. You know that."

Smiling, Dane replied, "I do know that. Thanks, man."

"Drive safely."

"Will do."

Then the line disconnected.

Grinning broadly, Dane returned his focus to the road.

Just as Dane had hoped, he arrived at the diner just as it was opening at five AM. In desperate need of a bathroom, a cup of coffee, and getting a chance to see his mate—not necessarily in that order—Dane swung off his bike and unbuckled his helmet. After locking it in a saddlebag, he headed inside.

Seeing Peggy—the same bigoted hostess from his first visit—behind the greeting stand, Dane swept his gaze over the place, but his mate was nowhere in sight.

He's probably in the back.

"Just one today, sir?" Peggy asked, her gaze sweeping over Dane as distaste filled her scent. She'd already picked up one menu and one bundle of napkin-wrapped silverware.

Dane ignored her attitude, figuring it stemmed from his rough appearance—helmet hair, chaps, boots, and jacket. "I'd

18

like to be placed in Danny's section, please." Considering there was only one other customer in the place, Dane figured there wouldn't be a problem with that.

"I'm sorry, sir," Peggy replied, her features pinching. "Danny doesn't work here anymore." There was a cold gleam in her eyes when she added, "He was unreliable and didn't show up for his shift yesterday. Young people these days." With a sniff, Peggy turned and indicated that he should follow her. "Let me assure you, Gloria is an excellent waitress. She'll treat you right."

"No, thank you."

Dane pivoted and headed out of the diner, his need to pee and desire for coffee momentarily forgotten. Pulling out his phone, he crossed to his motorcycle. He frowned, realizing that he'd never received an answer to his text to Danny the morning before. Dane had been so preoccupied with getting his paperwork finished, he hadn't even realized it. Then he hadn't called Danny the prior evening as he usually did because he'd been driving and had wanted to surprise him.

Okay. I have his address.

Deciding to head there, Dane rang Danny's number as he drove. Surprise filled him when it went straight to voicemail. He hoped his mate just had the phone off because he was sleeping in.

Dane found the house where Danny lived with his father. After shutting off his engine, he hesitated. If Danny was sleeping, he worried about waking him up . . . as well as the man's father.

Does the guy even know his son is gay? What if he's not out?

Except, with unease curling in his gut and his komodo dragon urging him onward, Dane swung off his bike. He'd apologize if he woke them or outed him.

I need to see my mate.

It took a good five minutes of persistent knocking before Dane heard movement on the other side of the door. When it opened, revealing an overweight dark-haired man, a wall of stale beer and BO smacked Dane in the face. The scent emanating from the house wasn't much better.

Damn. This is Danny's father?

"Whaddaya want?" the man slurred, obviously still drunk. He squinted at him through watery brown eyes. "Doncha know what time it is?"

"I'm looking for Danny," Dane stated. "Is he here?"

The man curled his lip into a sneer. "No, he ain't 'ere." He swayed as he swung his arm and pointed at Dane. "Ain't gonna have a useless faggot in my house."

"Where is he?" Dane demanded.

"Don't know and don't give a shit." Then the man stumbled back a few steps and slammed the door in Dane's face, all the while grumbling about faggots and assholes waking him too early.

Dane could have stopped the door from shutting, but unfortunately, he'd known the man was telling the truth. He didn't know and didn't care.

Returning to his motorcycle, Dane scrubbed a hand through his hair as uneasiness flooded him. Once more, he tried to call Danny, but again it went to voicemail. That time he left a message. Leaning against his motorcycle, Dane glanced up and down the street, but Danny didn't appear.

"Where are you, honey?"

Knowing he needed help, Dane did the only thing he could do and made another call.

"Do you have any fucking idea what time it is?"

Ignoring Delanrue's grumbled words, Dane stated, "I need help."

Sounding much more awake, Del asked, "What is it?"

"My mate is missing."

CHAPTER THREE

Hunching his shoulders against the chilly morning air, Danny focused on putting one tired foot in front of the other. His feet hurt, his legs ached, and his wrist throbbed. He saw a sign for a town in twelve miles and groaned under his breath.

Twelve miles. I can do it.

Danny tucked his casted right wrist against his chest and blinked against the tears threatening. Every step sent pain lancing through his broken wrist. He didn't know how his father had guessed the password to his phone, or even why, but when the man had read the sweet messages from Dane, he'd been beyond livid.

His father had used a wooden bat to not only break his phone but Danny's wrist when he'd lifted it to protect his head. The only thing that had saved him was his father being falling-down drunk . . . which he'd done — fall down. While the man had been trying to get up, Danny had been faster, even with agony coursing through his limb.

Running to his room, Danny had grabbed his wallet and fled through a window. He hadn't even had time to grab his hidden tip cash. Hearing his father lumbering his way, Danny hadn't wanted to take the chance.

Wonder when he'll find the tin canister on the shelf in the back of my closet. He'll think he hit the jackpot.

Every day after work, Danny would make certain he had somewhere between twenty and thirty bucks in his pockets. The rest of his tip money he would stick in his sock. When he would walk in the door, his father would demand his tip money, and he would empty his pockets for him.

Good thing for direct deposit.

Danny's paychecks were sent directly to the bank, but he saved up the remainder of his tip money for his monthly rent. Still, he had to have at least six hundred dollars in the canister.

And now it's all gone . . . just like Dane.

Thinking of the sexy man caused his heart to twist with sadness. When the nurse who'd helped him fill out the clinic paperwork—since Danny was right-handed—had asked if there was anyone she could call for him, Danny had wanted to contact Dane so very badly. Unfortunately, the man's number was in his phone, and that had been destroyed.

Shoulda memorized it.

Regret sat like a stone in Danny's belly. He would like to believe that if he'd called Dane, the man would have come. The sexy guy had been so sweet on the phone, always complimenting him and telling him he couldn't wait to see him again, not that he had actually given Danny a date as to when that would be.

Danny stumbled on a loose rock. Instinctively, he stretched out his arms . . . both of them. Shards of agony ripped up his right arm, and he cried out as he dropped to his knees. Black spots danced behind his vision.

Breathing deeply, Danny ignored the drops of moisture squeezing past his eyelids. He shivered as the rain-dampened earth soaked into the front of his pants. At least that gave him something to focus on other than the pulses radiating through him.

Blowing out a harsh breath, Danny lifted his head and stared at the tree-lined road stretching before him. He needed to get up. He needed to keep going.

Surely I can find a job somewhere that I can work with one arm for a while.

Spending the night in the hospital, Danny had completely

forgotten to call in sick to work. When he did remember—
mid-morning—he'd explained to the manager on duty, Gary,
that he'd broken his arm. Gary had been sympathetic, but
he'd also said the owner had a zero policy for no-shows.

Danny's job was toast.

After a few more calming breaths, Danny forced himself
back to his feet. He had to keep going. He had to get to the
next town. He needed a place to sit, eat a little, and think
about his next move.

Without a car, Danny wasn't certain where he was going
to sleep, either. He had a couple grand in the bank, but he was
loath to use it for hotels.

*I'll check the classifieds. Maybe I can find a cheap room or apart-
ment in the same place as a job.*

Groaning, Danny still had no idea what he could do one-
handed.

Danny walked, allowing his mind to drift. As it had done
for the last three days, his thoughts turned to Dane—big,
powerful, sexy Dane. He couldn't imagine that a guy like that
would be interested in his skinny ass, and now he was injured, homeless, and jobless.

Maybe it was for the best that he couldn't get in touch with
him.

Sighing sadly, Danny blinked away the moisture threatening the backs of his eyes. He clenched his left hand within the
confines of his jean jacket pocket. Shaking his head, he pushed
away thoughts of the handsome man.

"Okay," Danny whispered. "Focus on making a list of jobs.
Think, Daniel. Think."

Sadly, Danny's mind remained stubbornly blank.

Several hours later, Danny spotted the beginnings of a
town. The houses had been getting closer together, giving him
the much-needed boost to keep moving. He saw a sign for *The
Trophy Room Café* and nearly cried with relief.

Entering the place, Danny glanced around cautiously. He spotted a number of stuffed animal heads hanging on the walls as well as a few full-sized beasts. While he'd never hunted himself, Danny couldn't help but be impressed by whoever the taxidermist was. The cougar crouching on the log looked so very life-like.

And beautiful. And now I know why they call it The Trophy Room.

"Hey, sweetie. Sit wherever you like," an older woman greeted with a smile, coming toward him. As she drew nearer, her focus lingered on his casted arm and still-damp pants. "You okay?"

Giving the nice lady a small smile, Danny nodded. "Yeah," he murmured, making his way to a small table near the corner. "Just slipped on the road."

"Okay, then." She placed a laminated sheet before him. "You want somethin' hot to warm you up?"

"Yes, please." Not being a coffee drinker, Danny asked, "Do you have hot chocolate?"

"Sure do." With another smile, she added, "I'll whip that up for you and be back in a jiffy."

"Thank you," Danny whispered.

As she moved away, he turned his attention to the menu. The food was standard café fare — sandwiches, burgers, fries, and the like. Spotting the club sandwich, he felt his stomach gurgle.

When the waitress returned with not only the requested hot chocolate but a glass of water, Danny ordered the sandwich with tater tots. After she'd headed off again, he carefully pulled his pain pills from his pocket before frowning. They were in a slender prescription bottle with one of those child-proof lids. Unfortunately, Danny would need both hands to open it.

Grimacing, Danny peered around the table, wondering if he could press it against something, instead.

"You need a hand, sweetie?"

Danny hadn't heard the waitress approach and jolted in his seat, banging his wrist on the side of the table in the process. Pain shot up his arm, and he whimpered, a shudder working through him.

"Oh, dear. I'm so sorry." The woman rubbed up and down his back. "That was thoughtless of me. You musta really been deep in thought."

After letting out a deep breath, Danny forced a tremulous smile as he met her brown-eyed gaze. There was worry there, which he thought was nice.

"Sorry," Danny whispered. "Just, um, trying to figure out how to open that."

"Allow me." Without waiting, she reached out and picked up the bottle. "How'd you break your wrist" — she read the label — "Daniel?"

She popped the cap off the bottle and placed both items on the table.

Danny sighed, grimacing. "Defending myself from a baseball bat." The words were out of his mouth before he could censor himself.

Crapballs. I didn't even tell the nurse the truth.

While Danny knew he could have gotten the police involved, he didn't see the point. His father was the town drunk, and everyone had known it. Having his father tossed in jail would be pointless, because when he got out, he would be ten times worse the next time around.

Just better to leave.

"I sure hope the police catch whoever did it," she replied, looking troubled.

Meeting her concerned gaze, Danny lied, "It was an accident. Moved at the wrong time."

She hummed, her look telling Danny that she didn't believe him, but she didn't pursue it. "Well, you sit and relax. Warm up." Glancing outside, she shook her head. "It's gonna rain in a bit. Maybe you'd best rest a spell and let it pass."

"Thank you."

After she'd headed away again, Danny picked up the bottle and shook one of the pain pills onto the table. He wasn't a big fan of meds, but if he was going to be sitting and resting for a couple of hours, he felt safe enough to take one. After popping it into his mouth and swigging it back with some water, Danny stared at the open bottle and the lid. He shook out a second one before resealing the bottle and placing both into the pocket of his jeans.

Danny then focused on the hot chocolate. The rich, delicious beverage coated his tongue and throat perfectly. Sighing with pleasure, he relaxed for the first time since leaving his town's small clinic.

Eating became a lesson in patience. When he'd ordered the club sandwich, he hadn't thought about how he usually used two hands to hold it. After some thought, he squished it with his left hand to make it as thin as possible. It was still messy and fell apart a bit, but he enjoyed it anyway.

The tater tots were crispy and hot, fried to perfection. Their salty goodness burst over his taste buds. Mixed with a little ketchup, which added a hint of sweetness, his taste buds were in heaven.

To Danny's surprise, he managed to eat it all. By the time he finished, it was raining in earnest. He stared forlornly at the sheets of rain, grimacing. While the kindly old waitress had told him he could stay until it passed, Danny wasn't certain just how long that would be. He couldn't stay all afternoon. He needed to find a place to sleep.

Before Danny could decide what to do, the woman brought over a second hot chocolate. With a wink, she told him, "On the house."

Murmuring his thanks, Danny relaxed in his seat. While

his head felt just a bit swimmy from the pain meds, he realized his wrist had settled to a dull ache. Deciding to stop worrying—for a little bit, anyway—Danny sipped his fresh hot chocolate.

Soon enough, the rain stopped, and the sun came out.

Knowing his reprieve was up, Danny paid for his meal with his debit card.

"How far is the next town in that direction?" Danny asked the waitress while she rang him up.

Danny figured it was a little sad that he wasn't familiar with anywhere beyond the small town he'd left, but he'd never purchased a car. He hadn't had much in the way of friends, either, since his mother had homeschooled him. Danny had just finished his high school equivalency when she'd died in a car accident.

He'd been fifteen.

Then his father had started drinking.

Everything after that had been a tiresome slog to survive and begin scraping enough together to get the hell out of Dodge.

Well, I'm out. Now what do I do?

CHAPTER FOUR

"Do you have anything?" Dane didn't bother saying hello when he spotted Delanrue's number come up on his phone.

"Theo just texted me," Del stated. "He got a hit on Danny's debit card."

Dane knew Theo had been in the military before mating with Regales, and he was quite the tech guru. It made sense that Del had contacted the councilman and his mate. If he'd been thinking clearly, he should have done the same.

"Where?"

"I texted you the address. It's twenty miles south of your location," Del told him.

Twenty miles. My mate is twenty miles away. He'll be in my arms again soon.

Dane pulled out from under the gas station overhang where he'd been parked, waiting for a fall rainstorm to pass. Hell, even if it had still been raining, he would have headed out. He refused to wait another second.

"There's more, Dane."

Del's serious tone caused a fissure of worry to churn through Dane's gut. "Tell me," he demanded, bracing himself.

"Daniel Nunez was checked into that town's clinic overnight."

Sucking in a sharp breath, Dane asked the obvious. "Why?"

"Don't know," Del replied gruffly. "Their systems haven't

uploaded anything else, yet. Just his name. Maybe someone there is too busy to keep records up to date or just don't like using technology until they have to."

"Okay," Dane replied, carefully navigating the wet roads. "Thanks, Del. I'll keep you posted."

"Good. Fair warning." Amusement suddenly laced Del's voice. "Dakota is roaring your way on his bullet bike."

Dane huffed a soft laugh. "Well, I hope he doesn't think I'm going to entertain him after I find my mate."

"Naw," Del countered, chuckling quietly—something Dane had rarely heard his brother do before meeting Miggs. "I think he's got it in his head that if your mate can be found up there, maybe his is around there, too."

"Well, I hope whoever it may be isn't from Danny's town." Dane scowled as he shook his head. "They all seemed a little homophobic."

Del grunted. "Keep me posted."

"Will do."

Dane pulled up his messages and spotted Del's text. He linked it to his maps app and took a right at the first opportunity. Following the direction to the *Trophy Room Café* took almost fifteen more minutes on wet, windy roads, causing his patience to fray.

Spotting the small restaurant, Dane swiftly pulled into the parking lot. He inhaled deeply, but he caught no trace of his mate outside. Hurrying into the restaurant, he inhaled again . . . and nearly groaned.

Danny's scent hung heavy in the air, telling him he'd been there for some time and must have left only recently.

Probably right after he paid.

An older woman appeared from the back, probably drawn by the bell on the door that had chimed when he'd entered. She smiled and called, "Just sit where ya like. Can I getcha some coffee?"

"No, thank you, ma'am," Dane replied politely. He needed

information, and he recalled the old adage about how you catch more flies with honey. "I'm looking for a friend of mine. Danny. About five-foot-eight. Short, light-brown hair. Hazel eyes." Dane really wished he'd had the presence of mind to take a picture of his mate that first day, but he'd been too over-whelmed by his intoxicating scent. "I think he was here just recently."

The woman's eyes narrowed, and her chin lifted a little. She glanced toward the pair of men who were at a table by the window. They were her only other customers, but she still lowered her voice.

"You ain't the one who took a bat to his arm, are ya?"

Dane's gut clenched, and he drew in a harsh breath. "No," he denied softly. Thrusting his hand through his hair, he mumbled, "That explains the clinic. Why didn't he call me?"

The woman's features softened a bit. "You his brother or somethin'?"

Nodding, Dane replied, "Or something." Since she still didn't look convinced, he added, "Please. I need to see for my-self that he's okay. Do you know where he went?"

For another moment, the woman just stared at him. Finally, she pointed. "He walked outta town that way."

"Thank you so much," Dane rumbled, nodding as he backed up. "I truly appreciate it."

She nodded back before turning her attention back to her customers.

Dane rushed from the café and hopped back on his bike. Firing it up, he headed in the direction the woman had indi-cated. He scanned the stretch of road that appeared around each bend even as he kept inhaling the fresh mountain air.

Finally, his mate's faint scent tantalized his senses. Eager-ness flooded him, knowing that he was growing closer. His animal rumbled in the back of his mind, urging him to go even faster.

Rounding a bend, Dane spotted a figure in the distance. He noticed a slight limp in the step of the hunched figure. Slowing his bike, he still couldn't help but admire Danny's slender frame, although he didn't like the tight lines across his shoulders. He also had his right arm tucked forward with his left shoved into his pocket. Danny's focus was downward, as if he watched each step he took.

Even when Dane slowed to an almost idle so he could ride next to him, Danny still didn't look up. Instead, he appeared to hunch even tighter in on himself. The acrid tinge of fear colored his scent.

That won't do.

"Danny," Dane called. "Danny, honey. Stop."

Danny froze for an instant. Then his head snapped up. He stared at Dane with wide, disbelieving eyes.

"D-Dane?" Danny blinked, as if he thought he was seeing things and Dane would disappear.

Stopping his bike, Dane quickly pulled his helmet from his head. He forced a wide smile even as the cast on his mate's arm damn near broke his heart. After setting the helmet on the handlebar, Dane swung off the bike.

"Hey, Danny," Dane crooned, reaching for his mate. Easing his arms around his waist gently, mindful of his injury, he dipped his head and bussed a kiss to Danny's temple. "Why didn't you call me, honey? What happened?"

Danny stared up at him in shock for a couple more heartbeats. Then he lifted his good hand and rested it on Dane's chest. "You're here," he whispered, sliding his fingers over the leather jacket. "But how?"

"I'll answer your questions if you answer mine," Dane teased, smiling at his mate. Then he heard a car coming and glanced toward it. "But not here. Not on the side of the road." Returning his focus to Danny, Dane skimmed one hand up his back so he could thread his fingers through the short strands of his mate's hair. "Will you come with me? We'll find a nice hotel, curl up together, and answer all each other's questions."

Although Danny glanced at Dane's bike with a hint of trepidation, he still nodded.

Dane did a mental fist-pump.

Yes!

Moving toward his bike, Dane opened the rear saddlebag. He pulled out the helmet and eased it onto Danny's head. After strapping it into place, Dane pulled out the leather jacket. He took in the cast on Danny's wrist, which covered most of his fingers to just below his elbow.

"Just one arm for now," Dane decided, lifting the jacket and moving behind Danny. "Left arm in, and we'll tuck the other to your chest."

Doing as Dane had bidden, Danny slipped on the leather jacket. "You came prepared."

"I did," Dane confirmed as he settled the jacket on Danny's shoulders. "I was hoping you'd agree to ride with me." Ever-so-carefully, Dane zipped up the bottom just a little, holding the jacket in place. "Now then. Let's get you up here."

Dane gripped Danny's waist and pinned a serious look on his mate. "I'm going to lift you onto the back of the bike." He quickly pointed at a piece of curved metal, which was part of the frame, before gripping his waist again. "That's a good spot for you to grip. Ready?"

Danny scoffed softly. "You can't really lift me onto the bike. Can you?"

"I so can," Dane assured with a playful wink. "Rest your good hand on my shoulder."

While Danny still looked skeptical, he did as he'd been told.

Dane tightened his hold and, with his increased shifter strength, easily hefted Danny onto the back seat. "Put your feet on the pedals," he instructed, waiting. "There we go."

Once Danny was situated on the motorcycle's bitch seat,

Dane eased his hold. He swung his leg over his own seat. "I'm going to tilt it upright." From the look Dane had seen Danny give his ride, he guessed his human had never been on one before. "You can keep hanging onto the bike frame, or you can grab my jacket or belt loops. Whatever makes you most comfortable." Then Dane brought his bike to life.

Turning his head as he buckled his own helmet, Dane asked, "Ready?"

"O-Okay."

Not a ringing endorsement, but Dane would take it. "Don't worry, honey. I'll keep you safe."

Starting off slow, Dane trundled down the road. He turned his head a little to scent his mate, keeping track of his emotions. While there was a bit of fear hanging around him, there was more pain mixed with disbelief.

I can work with that.

Dane didn't try to talk to Danny. There would be time enough for that later. Instead, he focused on keeping his mate comfortable with his ride.

Before too long, Dane smiled, noting that the fear had dissipated.

Nice.

Spotting the sign for a chain hotel, Dane slowed and turned into the parking lot. He stopped in front of the door marked *Office* and settled the bike on the kickstand. Dane carefully hopped off his motorcycle and turned to Danny.

"Stay here," Dane urged, touching Danny's chin. "I'm going to get a room. Be right back."

Dane didn't wait for a reply. He hurried into the office and found a bored-looking woman behind the desk. When Dane asked for two rooms, she perked up a little, but he ignored her flirty smile.

After taking both keycards in their paper sleeves with the room numbers written on them, Dane returned to the motorcycle. "Hang onto these."

Seeing Danny nibble his bottom lip and the way his brows furrowed, Dane knew his beautiful mate had gotten the wrong idea, too. He eased back onto the bike as he made his way to the two rooms—side by side on the ground floor—he smiled. Dane would explain soon enough.

Once Dane had parked before room one-twenty-six, he again eased off the motorcycle. "Ready to be lifted down?" he asked, turning to face the man he hoped to soon make his lover.

Well, depending on his injury.

Danny nibbled his bottom lip once more as he nodded, and Dane swallowed a groan. He wanted to do a little nibbling of his own. His cock ached behind the fly of his jeans, but he knew they had to do some talking first.

Damn.

"Okay." Dane gripped Danny's waist again and helped him from the motorcycle. Once his human stood on his own two feet, he slipped one arm around Danny's waist and guided him toward the door. "Let's get you comfortable. Then I'll come back for my bag."

That was when Dane realized that Danny hadn't had a bag on him. Didn't he take any stuff from home?

Something else to ask about.

After taking the appropriate keycard from Danny, Dane opened the door. Then he guided his mate inside. The room was typical for what he'd asked for—a king-bed suite with a jetted tub—so it contained a sitting area and a large bed. The jetted tub, however, was in the main area, not the bathroom, which contained a shower.

Nice.

Dane could see them relaxing in the tub together after a round of vigorous claiming, watching some inane TV show while sharing their secrets. His gaze fell to Danny's wrist once more. He realized he would need to get plastic bags to wrap around his mate's cast.

"Um, I figure this must be your room," Danny whispered, shifting from foot to foot. He started toward the door. "I'll go to the other room."

"No, honey." Dane gripped Danny's shoulder lightly, drawing his attention. "This is *our* room." He tossed the keycard on a side table before plucking the second envelope from Danny's fingers and placing it there, too. "That card is for my brother, Dakota. He's on his way, so I got him a room, too."

"Y-Your brother?" Danny's brows furrowed. "Was that the big guy who was at the café with you?"

Dane shook his head. "No. That guy's name is Austin. He's an associate of mine." Guiding Danny to a comfortable-looking sofa, he told him, "My brother is Dakota. He's younger by a couple of years. You'll meet my older brother, Delanrue, when we get back to Savannah."

"Savannah?"

Realizing he was jumping ahead, Dane chuckled softly to cover his slip. "Have a seat. Let me grab my stuff and lock up my bike. Then we'll order take out from somewhere and talk. Sound good?"

Relief filled Dane when he saw Danny's nod. Hurrying out of the room, he flipped the latch on the door so it couldn't close. Then he grabbed his duffle bag from the right saddlebag. After locking them all, Dane returned to the room.

Dane saw that Danny hadn't moved . . . much. He still sat on the sofa, although he'd removed both the leather and jean jackets, but his focus was pinned on the coffee table before him. He didn't even react when Dane placed his bags on a nearby chair.

After removing his helmet and placing it on the table, Dane scrubbed his hands through his shaggy blond hair, easing the itches. Now that he'd stopped moving and had his mate safely with him, he felt the fatigue from driving all night begin to creep into his psyche. Doing his best to beat it back, he thought about using the complimentary coffee machine.

"How did you find me?" Danny suddenly asked, lifting his gaze to Dane. "What are you doing here?"

Okay, that wasn't what Dane had originally thought Danny would ask, but they were certainly valid questions.

Crossing to the coffee table, Dane settled on it. He bracketed Danny's knees with his own. Needing to touch, he reached out and cradled Danny's good hand between both of his own.

"I drove all night because I wanted to surprise you at the diner first thing this morning," Dane admitted, squeezing Danny's hand lightly. "Imagine my shock when Peggy said you no longer worked there."

Grimacing, Danny mumbled, "I bet she loved telling you that."

"You'd win that bet," Dane whispered before lifting his mate's fingers to his lips and kissing his knuckles lightly. "And I came because I wanted to spend time with you." Giving Danny a playful smile, Dane added, "You did promise me a date." Sobering, Dane couldn't help but ask again, "Now." He touched Danny's fingers to his lips again, holding his mate's gaze. "Why didn't you call me?"

CHAPTER FIVE

Danny's heart was beating so fast he could barely take a full breath. He could still hardly believe that Dane was there, with him, even though he was sitting right in front of him, holding his hand so reverently. Danny had wanted to see Dane again so badly.

And now he's here.

Finding his tongue, Danny admitted, "My phone was smashed, and I hadn't memorized your phone number."

"Ah," Dane hummed. A smile teased at the corners of his full lips. "We do rely a bit heavily on our technology these days, don't we?"

Danny nodded, hearing no censure in Dane's tone.

Then Dane's brows furrowed. "How did your phone get smashed?" He glanced pointedly at Danny's wrist before meeting his gaze again. "Did this happen at the same time?"

Sighing deeply, Dane nodded again. "Yeah."

"Will you tell me what happened?"

Dane's dark eyes entreated him to talk, to share.

"I must have left my phone out." Danny frowned, still confused as to how that had happened. Then something clicked. "Or maybe he went searching for it."

"Who?" Dane pressed.

Holding Dane's gaze, Danny admitted, "My dad. He saw our messages, and well, I guess assuming you have a gay son is different than actually finding proof." Danny grimaced while shaking his head, recalling his father's drunken rage. "He came at me with a bat."

A low, feral-sounding growl rumbled from Dane's throat. Danny watched his jaw tightening as a muscle ticked on one side. His eyes narrowed, and for just an instant, Danny thought his pupils appeared more slit-like . . . like a snake's. Then Dane blinked, and it was gone.

Bowing his head, Dane whispered, "I'm so sorry I wasn't there to protect you." He lifted his gaze to Danny's once more. "So he tossed you out after attacking you?" When Danny nodded, Dane pressed, "With nothing but the clothes on your back?"

Danny nibbled his bottom lip before admitting, "He didn't so much toss me out as I had to flee. I knew he would —" Pulling his hand away, Danny rubbed at his chest.

"Knew he would what?" Dane pressed softly, touching his knees gently with his strong hands.

His own father. He just knew it. "He would have killed me," he whispered. "He was aiming for my head."

Dane sucked in a harsh breath as another hissing growl sounded through the room. Just as quickly, he reached over and grabbed Danny. Dane tugged him off the sofa, and Danny suddenly found himself on Dane's lap, clutched in a tight embrace. Dane tucked his face against Danny's neck, and he just seemed to be breathing in his scent . . . which couldn't be all that good, because he hadn't showered since the day before, and he'd done a lot of walking.

Confused, Danny rubbed his good hand up and down Dane's arm. He was relieved that the big man had turned him in such a way so his injured arm wasn't caught between them. Instead, Danny's shoulder rested against Dane's broad chest, allowing the other man easy access to his neck.

"Why isn't that fucker in jail?" Dane rumbled gruffly, anger filling his tone. "He was at home this morning. Why?"

Danny gasped. "Y-You went to my house?"

Well, guess it's not mine anymore, is it?

Dane lifted his head and met his gaze squarely. "After you

weren't at the diner, yes. I started looking for you."

"H-He's my father," Danny whispered.

After issuing a deep sigh, Dane mumbled, "So you didn't press charges."

Danny nodded.

Dane opened his mouth, but the ring of his phone caused him to snap it closed just as quickly. Pulling out the phone, he peered at the screen. He held Danny's gaze as he accepted the call and lifted the device to his ear.

"I found him," Dane stated to . . . whoever.

Being on Dane's lap, Danny was close enough to hear a deep voice say, "Good. Theo said you checked into a hotel. I'm assuming he's with you?"

As Dane's lips twitched a little, he confirmed. "He is."

"Why two rooms?" the speaker asked. "Planning to be all noble and shit?"

Dane smirked. "Not a snowball's chance in hell. The second room is for Dakota."

The man on the other end of the line grunted before saying, "I sent the address to Dakota. He's close. What room are you in? Or should he go to the office to get his key?"

"We're in one-twenty-six."

"I'll let him know." For a second, there was silence, and Dane began lowering his phone. Then the man said, "Congratulations, Dane."

A relieved-looking smile curved Dane's lips as he stared into Danny's eyes. "Thanks, Del. Talk soon."

"Sounds good. Contact me if you need anything else."

"And thank Theo for me, would ya," Dane continued. "I couldn't have found Danny without him."

"Will do."

Then Dane placed the phone on the coffee table beside him. "That was Delanrue. Del. He's my older brother."

"The one I'll meet when we go to Savannah?" Danny

guessed, recalling what Dane had said earlier. "You're just assuming."

"I am," Dane confirmed, bringing his hand up and sliding his finger through Danny's hair. "You were injured while away from me, and I need to take care of you. I—" His eyes narrowed, and his features tightened for a few seconds. When his smile returned, Dane stated, "There is so much for me to explain."

Danny just bet there was. *Like*—"You told your brother to thank a guy named Theo. That he helped you find me." Still confused on that point, he pressed, "How did he do that?"

Dane began rubbing his hand along Danny's spine in slow, rhythmic strokes. His expression turned a bit guarded as he admitted, "Theo was in the military, and he's very good with computers." After clearing his throat in discomfort, Dane admitted, "When I couldn't find you, I gave Del your information, and he passed it on to Theo. He couldn't track you through your cell, which makes sense, since it was destroyed." Letting out a deep breath, Dane admitted, "He tracked your debit card usage."

Gaping, Danny tensed. "Y-You guys can do that?" He shook his head. "That's so illegal."

Dane's smile appeared entreating. "I had to find you."

"A-Are you part of the mob?" Danny hissed the question. Just as quickly, he shook his head and attempted to rise off Dane's lap. "No. No, I don't want to know."

Holding Danny steady, Dane didn't release him. Instead, he rubbed over his back and side as he crooned, "Not the mob. You're safe. I'd never hurt you."

Danny didn't know if he believed Dane's words, but it was the pain filling the man's deep brown eyes that called to him, making him cease his struggling. For some reason, Danny just knew that his doubt hurt Dane. He just couldn't figure out why. They barely knew each other.

Before more could be said, a knock sounded at their door.

Dane sighed before easing Danny back onto the sofa. Rising, he headed toward the door. After checking the peephole, he opened it and admitted another blond — and while his hair was cut a bit shorter and he stood maybe an inch shorter — he looked so similar that the man could only be Dane's brother, Dakota.

After greeting Dane with a one-armed hug, Dakota held up a couple of paper sacks with a chain restaurant logo on them. "Brought food. Figured you guys might be hungry." Then he turned a big, friendly smile Danny's way. "Hey, man. Glad we tracked ya down. Poor Dane was damn fit to be tied when he couldn't find ya." As Dakota placed the yummy-smelling bags on the table, his gaze must have noticed Danny's cast. Growling, he glanced from Dane to Danny and back again. "Someone hurt your mate?" he snarled. "Who? Who do we need to kill?"

A fresh burst of unease spiked through Danny, and he shifted farther away from the pair.

Dane groaned as he shook his head. "Gods, Dakota. I had just about managed to convince him that we are *not* part of the mob." Pushing the coffee table out of the way, Dane dropped to his knees beside Danny. "Honey, please calm down. We're not the mob."

Dakota appeared genuinely confused. "We're not the mob." He glanced between them once more. "You haven't explained anything?"

Sighing deeply, Dane continued to stare at Danny while answering Dakota's question. "We've only been here for twenty minutes or so. We haven't gotten into everything, yet."

"Okay." Dakota's grin once again turned friendly. "Really, Danny. We're not the mob." Waggling his eyebrows, he added, "We're way cooler."

Danny didn't know if he should laugh at the brother's antics or go lock himself in the bathroom. "I . . . um —"

"Do you want help explaining?" Dakota asked, resting his hands on his hips. "I could show him while you hold him so he doesn't run screaming for the hills."

Unable to help himself, fear spiked through Danny. If they weren't part of the mob, what were they? Assassins? Was Dane supposed to hold him down while Dakota cut him or something?

"Holy fucking shit, Kota," Dane snarled, glaring at his brother. "That's not being helpful."

If Danny's terror wasn't growing, he would have thought the confused look on the big man's face was funny. As it was, it finally hit him. He was in a strange place, with people he didn't know, and no one would even care or look for him if he ended up missing . . . or dead.

A whimper escaped him.

"Gods, Dane." Dakota backed up a couple of steps, his hands lifting in placation. "I didn't mean to freak him out." His attention turned to Danny. "Really, Danny. We would never, ever hurt you. You're Dane's mate. You're special. He's been waiting for you for almost two centuries."

Wait. What?

Hearing that odd comment pulled Danny out of his growing panic faster than he thought possible. "Two centuries," he whispered, frowning as he glanced from Dane to Dakota and back again. Dane sported a beseeching expression where he continued to kneel beside him, his hands lifted as if wanting to touch but uncertain of his welcome. Dakota rested his fists on his hips and stood glaring at the carpet. "What the hell are you talking about?"

Dane sighed deeply before rising to his feet. "I'm going to lose the leathers and give you a little space to breathe, Danny," he whispered, peering at him with an uncertain expression on his face. "Then I'll explain everything." Glaring at his brother, Dane muttered, "Even though I'd *hoped* to have the chance to woo him first."

Dakota appeared chagrined as he rubbed the back of his neck. "Sorry, bro."

Danny watched warily as Dane did just that, revealing the form-fitting jeans beneath the black leather.

Wow. So sexy.

Then Dane removed his leather jacket. He followed that up by taking off the sweater underneath, leaving him in nothing but a black t-shirt. The fabric stretched across his massive torso, highlighting his defined pectorals, bulging biceps, and ripped abdominals.

Just wow again.

Finally, Dane took off his boots and socks, leaving him in jeans, a shirt, and barefoot.

Danny couldn't figure out why that was sexy, but it was. Despite the odd and slightly scary situation, his dick began to fill. It certainly didn't care that these two huge men could easily make him disappear from the face of the planet.

"Do you want me to go, bro?" Dakota asked softly, scratching the back of his neck. "I obviously keep putting my foot in my mouth." Grimacing, he admitted, "I kinda did the same thing with Sin. I just don't seem to be able to explain shifters to humans without saying dumb shit."

Dane sighed deeply before casting a slight smile on his brother. "You mean well." Waving his hand to the forgotten bags of food, he added, "Take your jacket off and join us. You did bring the food, after all."

Dakota cleared his throat and nodded. "Okay." Then he began getting more comfortable, too.

Reaching for the food, Dane began pulling out paper-wrapped burgers and cartons of fries. "So, yes, I'm a lot older than I look." He pushed a burger toward Danny while taking one for himself. "And as Dakota insinuated. I'm not human. Neither of us are."

"Not . . . human?"

Danny cocked his head. His stomach grumbled, even though he didn't think it had been that long ago that he'd eaten the club sandwich. A glance at the clock on the nightstand told him he was mistaken. That had been hours ago.

"Soooo, you're . . . aliens?" Danny guessed, unwrapping the burger one-handed. "Are you really hiding a lizard face and you eat live mice?"

He'd seen that on a TV show once.

To Danny's surprise, the brothers exchanged a clearly surprised look.

Dakota actually grinned. "How'd you know about us being lizards?" Leaning closer, he openly sniffed. "You smell totally human."

"Uuuuhhhhh—" Danny had no idea what he was supposed to say to that.

"I think he was kidding, Dakota." Dane's voice came out soft, a low soothing rumble. "And no, we're not aliens. We were born right here on earth, just almost two centuries ago. Our kind are quite long-lived." Before Danny had to come up with a response to that, Dane asked, "Have you ever heard the term paranormals before?"

Danny decided to give that the thought it deserved. He took a big bite of burger and chewed slowly. Enjoying the mouthful, he took his time before swallowing.

"I've seen those paranormal ghost shows on TV before," Danny began slowly, glancing between the brothers. "Where they go into haunted houses to explain sightings and stuff."

Shaking his head, Dane countered, "I'm talking about beings that people consider myth or legend." After a second of hesitation, he explained, "Shapeshifters, vampires, gargoyles, demons, angels, fae. That sort of thing."

Danny scowled at Dane. "Um, I was too busy with home-work growing up to read fairy tales." He saw Dane's brows lift, so he continued, "Then after Mom died, I was too busy staying out of Dad's way and earning my own money so I could eat."

"Gods, honey," Dane murmured. "I'm so sorry that hap-pened to you." His gaze flicked to Danny's wrist. "So very much."

"Is that who hurt him?" Dakota jumped in, anger entering his voice. "His dad?"

Dane nodded once. "Yes."

Putting down his burger, Dakota cracked his knuckles. "You sure I can't kill him?"

Frowning at Dakota, Dane stated, "I know that's the shifter way, Kota, but the man is human. We can't kill him for harm-ing my Fate-given mate."

Dakota grumbled under his breath, "No one would ever find the body."

Unable to help himself, Danny barked a laugh, although it sounded a bit hysterical, even to his own ears.

These men are . . . insane.

Why do all the sexy ones have to be taken or crazy?

Danny also wondered what it would take to get away from them. Even as he thought that, his heart twinged with regret. He'd really hoped Dane would be one of the good ones.

Story of my life.

CHAPTER SIX

Dane could smell the disbelief, unease, and fear radiating off Danny in potent waves. His komodo dragon rumbled with unease in his mind. He agreed with his animal.

They were going about this all wrong.

Sighing deeply, Dane racked his brain for another approach. Grabbing a French fry, he popped it into his mouth and chewed. He hadn't eaten since the day before — being too eager to return to his mate, then finding him gone had distracted him — and his stomach rumbled. Dane ate a couple of bites of his burger, watching Danny do the same.

Each time Dakota opened his mouth, Dane shook his head, and his brother snapped his mouth closed.

Good.

Dane loved his brother. He truly did, but the man was right. He really did know how to put his foot in his mouth around human mates. His explaining skills sucked.

Del got lucky, having a shifter mate.

Pushing the uncharitable thought from his mind, Dane refocused on Danny. His human was damn perfect for him. He knew it in his heart already.

Once Dane had finished his first burger, he wiped his fingers on a napkin, cleaning off the grease. "So," he began quietly. "I listed a number of paranormal species, and I can tell that probably wasn't the correct approach." Forcing a tight smile, Dane focused on Danny and his wary expression. "You don't believe a word I'm saying, and that's okay. There's a reason there's the saying, seeing is believing."

Danny's eyes narrowed, but he didn't say anything.

That was fine.

"My brothers and I are part of the species known as shifters." Dane figured it would be easier just to lay out the basics. "We share our psyche with an animal, and we can turn into that animal at will. We're—"

"Prove it," Danny cut in. When Dane hesitated, he arched one brow. "You did say, seeing is believing."

"I did." Dane turned to look at Dakota. "Maybe your idea had merit after all."

Dakota swallowed his bite of burger before asking, "Which one?"

Dane shrugged. "You shift. I'll hold him so he can't run or just in case he passes out."

Grabbing a napkin with his free hand, Dakota placed his burger on the wrapper. As he wiped his fingers clean, he glanced around the space. "Good thing you got a suite. We'll need to move some furniture a bit." He smirked. "Too bad we don't have Del and Miggs here. Miggs is a cute little guinea pig shifter. No way anyone would be scared of him."

Dane chuckled as he nodded. "Very true." Then he rose to his feet, grabbed the edge of the coffee table, and pulled it off to the side.

Dakota did the same with the chair he'd been sitting in. Then he bent and began removing his boots.

Focusing on Danny, Dane took in his incredulous expression. Ignoring that, he knelt before his mate once more. "My brother and I share our spirit with a komodo dragon. We're pretty darn big, and we can be lethal to our enemies." Hearing Danny's breathing become harsher, Dane quickly cradled his good hand between both of his own. "But you will never be in any danger from any of us. We are still sentient in our animal forms. We know who our friends are, our family, and our loved ones. Neither me nor my brothers would ever, *ever* hurt you."

Dane didn't know how to express that sentiment enough.

"You really believe your turn into . . . animals?"

Obviously, Danny just couldn't wrap his brain around that concept. That was okay. Most humans couldn't . . . at least, not right away.

Nodding, Dane urged Danny to his feet. "Let's go sit on the other side of the bed. That'll give us a bit of separation from him. Hopefully, you won't be scared that way." Komodo dragons were big animals to begin with, and as was pretty standard for shifters, they were larger than natural ones.

To Dane's relief, Danny obeyed his urging. He guided him to the far end of the suite. After settling on the bed, his back to the headboard, Dane urged Danny to rest between his spread thighs. Holding his mate to his chest, Dane felt his own dragon rumble happily in his mind.

While neither of them liked the continued disbelief and tension flooding Danny's scent, they appreciated that their mate was safe in their arms.

Dakota had his shirt off and hesitated with his hands near the fly of his jeans. "Okay, uh, at the risk of sounding prudish, you're not bonded yet," he pointed out. "I betcha you don't want your mate to see my assets, and I don't wanna piss off my brother. Toss me a pillow."

As a rule, shifters didn't really have a problem with nudity. Shifting with clothes on was hard on the threads, after all. Dane and his brothers had seen each other naked more times than he remembered.

Except, as Dane thought about Danny seeing his brother — *Yep, he's right.*

Reaching over, Dane grabbed a pillow and tossed it to Dakota. His brother caught it in one hand and held it in front of his groin. He obviously unzipped using the other hand, for a few seconds later, he kicked off his jeans. Then Dakota crouched on the floor.

"Now remember," Dakota stated. "I'm still Dane's brother no matter what form I take, and you are his Fate-given mate. I would never hurt you and would even protect you should you need it."

Dane could see Danny's flushed cheeks and scented his embarrassment. He nibbled his bottom lip, and he appeared to be staring at the comforter rather than Dakota. His sweet mate had obviously not been around too many naked men.

Then Dane remembered Danny's admission in the bathroom.

My mate is a virgin.

Waving a hand in Dakota's direction, Dane ordered, "Hurry up, bro. Let's get this part over with."

Dakota nodded, then started his shift. As Council Enforcers, they all practiced their shift on a regular basis, keeping the process swift and seamless. Even as the sound of bones popping and tendons cracking filled the room, it didn't last long.

Within a few seconds, Dakota's thickly muscled body had expanded. His skin darkened to a greenish-brown hue and turned to thick leather. He grew a long tail, and his hair disappeared as his head reshaped.

A komodo dragon formed in their hotel suite.

"Oh my god," Danny squeaked. For a second, he struggled in Dane's hold. "No, no, no. Gotta—"

"Relax, Danny," Dane crooned, holding his mate close. "That's Dakota, remember? We told you. You wanted proof. He won't hurt you."

Danny continued to shake his head, his limbs flailing. He let out a pain-filled cry before clutching his casted limb to his chest. A heartbeat later, he slumped against Dane's chest.

Gently palming Danny's jaw, Dane tipped his head back. He saw his mate's eyes were closed, and he breathed in long, slow breaths. His long black lashes fanned over his cheeks, giving him an angelic look.

Sighing, Dane pressed a chaste kiss to his temple before re-turning Danny's head to his chest. By the time he returned his focus to Dakota, his brother had returned to his human form. He was pulling on his jeans, and a frown curved his lips.

"I'm sorry, Dane," Dakota toned, straightening and zip-ping his jeans.

Dane gave his brother a half-shrug. "It's not anything we didn't expect."

Even as Dakota nodded, he still appeared troubled. "What are you gonna do now?"

What indeed?

A jaw-cracking yawn took him.

"I think Danny has the right idea. I'm going to curl up un-der the covers with my mate and take a nap. I'll try again when he wakes up."

Dakota nodded. He pulled his shirt over his head and stuffed his feet into his boots. After shoving his socks into a pocket, Dakota glanced around the place. "Del said you got me a room?"

Dane nodded, pointing. "Just next door. The key is there."

Picking up the envelope, Dakota shoved it into a back pocket. Then he grabbed another burger as well as a carton of fries. He headed toward the door, pausing with his hand on the handle.

"I'll be next door if you need me," Dakota told him.

Smiling at his brother, Dane nodded. "I know. Thanks, bro."

Dakota waved the hand holding the food as he stepped out. "Get some rest."

With a sigh, Dane eased from the bed. He rounded the large mattress and pulled down the blanket and sheet on the far side. Leaning over, he carefully pulled Danny across the bed, removed his shoes and socks, and tucked him in. Then Dane cleaned up the food, putting it into the mini-fridge. Fi-nally, he locked the door and shut off the lights.

After a second of hesitation, Dane pulled his shirt from his body and unbuttoned the top button of his jeans, but left them in place. It wasn't the most comfortable way to sleep, but he didn't want his mate to be uncomfortable upon waking either. Dane toyed with the idea of removing some of Danny's clothes but kept it limited to his footwear.

Climbing in on the other side, Dane eased close to Danny. He slid his arms around his mate's pliant body, holding him close, and let out a deep sigh. The day certainly hadn't turned out anything like he'd hoped.

May the Fates offer guidance in my dreams.

Then Dane allowed his body to relax and his mind to drift.

Something tugged at Dane's subconscious, pulling him from the most wonderful of dreams. He had his mate in his arms. They were cuddling close, his body all warm and willing. Dane didn't want to let it go, wishing for a few more minutes in that wonderful place.

Except, the sound of a soft thud and a whimper cut through his peace.

Sliding his arm across empty sheets, Dane realized something was wrong.

I went to bed with my mate in my arms.

That hadn't been a dream.

Cracking open his eyelids, Dane took in the room. The lights were still off, but his shifter eyesight still allowed him to make out every detail. He noticed the tell-tale glow under the door to the bathroom, telling him where his mate was.

Just as Dane thought about pushing the sheet aside and checking on him, the light was turned off, and the door opened. He waited, watching. A second later, Danny crept from the room, his shoes on his feet and his jean jacket around his shoulders.

Danny tiptoed across the suite, obviously heading toward the door.

Pain unlike anything Dane had ever experienced before stabbed through him. His mate was leaving him. He swallowed hard, squashing it down hard.

He's just scared.

The stench of fear permeated the room now that the bathroom door had been opened.

"Danny, honey," Dane rumbled softly, hoping not to startle his mate.

The human's squeak and how he spun told Dane that he hadn't succeeded.

Sighing softly, Dane sat up in bed. "Leaving without giving me a chance to explain?" He leaned over and flicked on the nightstand lamp, illuminating the room in a soft glow.

Danny gaped at him for a few seconds, his gaze roving over Dane's chest. The scent of arousal began to beat out the smell of fear. Dane would have been proud, but he knew it wouldn't last.

Snapping his gaze to Dane's face, Danny whispered, "You're not human."

"Correct," Dane agreed. "You didn't believe us. You wanted proof." He gauged the distance between them. While Dane knew he could reach his human before he could open the door, he didn't want to keep his mate by force. "We agreed and gave you that proof. Won't you give me a chance to explain now that we've done as you asked?" After a second of hesitation, Dane added, "Please?"

This was his mate, and he wasn't too proud to beg.

Dane could see Danny's indecision. It was written all over his face. He nibbled his bottom lip, tightening his hold on his jean jacket, then his arm relaxed again.

Finally, Danny whispered, "Why did you tell me? What do you want with me?"

Okay. Questions. That's a good start.

Dane sure hoped so anyway. Smiling at his beautiful human, he reminded, "We said we were long-lived. Do you recall?"

Danny responded with a jerky nod.

"Do you remember how old Dakota said I was?"

After licking his tongue over his bottom lip—*and gods, I want to trace that path with my own tongue*—Danny replied, "He said you were almost two centuries old."

Dane held Danny's gaze as he admitted, "I'm one hundred eighty-two years old. Shifters can live upward of five hundred, so technically, I'm not even middle age, yet."

Danny gaped, his jaw sagging open as his eyes widened. His mouth formed the word *wow*, although no sound came out.

"You asked why we told you, what I wanted from you," Dane continued, praying what he revealed next wouldn't be the straw that broke the camel's back, so to speak.

After Danny had nodded, Dane told him, "It can get lonely living such a long life, so Fate gives each paranormal a mate, a soul mate. That person complements them, completes them, and are damn near perfect for them." Lifting a hand, Dane indicated Danny. "For me, that mate is you. I'm telling you this because I want the opportunity to get to know you, to hold you, to cherish you, to bond with you, and to love you the way you deserve for the rest of our lives."

Dane closed his mouth and waited. He knew there were only two possibilities. Either Danny would walk out that door, forcing Dane to do his best to care for him from afar, or Danny would ask questions.

A long minute passed before Danny turned toward the door.

Clenching his jaw, Dane fought his urge to call him back.

Danny reached the door. His good hand hovered over the lock for several seconds, seemingly frozen. Then he turned.

The two words Danny whispered sent a fresh wave of hope

through Dane's chest.

"Why me?"

CHAPTER SEVEN

Waking in Dane's arms had been one of the most amazing experiences of Danny's life . . . right up until he recalled why he'd passed out in the first place.

Shock.

Danny had seen a man turn into an animal. That sort of shit just wasn't supposed to be possible. He'd lain there as his pulse spiked and his breathing sped up for a reason other than the sexy man wrapped around him like an octopus.

Who knew the sexy man — monster — would turn out to be a snuggler?

Okay, that's not fair. Dane's never been anything but kind . . . sexy . . . hawt . . . sweet . . . patient.

Erg! But his brother turned into a frickin' dinosaur, and he said he could do it, too!

Panic racing through him, Danny had thought only of getting away. He needed space — time — somewhere to hide.

To that end, Danny had wriggled — literally, since even a sleeping Dane didn't seem to want to release him — out of the bed. He'd been relieved . . . sort of . . . to discover he was still fully clothed. Once he'd spotted his shoes, he'd hurried to the bathroom to take care of business and pull on his footwear.

Danny had been halfway across the dark room when Dane had revealed that he was awake. Seeing the hurt in his expression had caused Danny's gut to twist uncomfortably. He'd had the unexpected urge to go to the man, to soothe and comfort him.

Why?

While Danny knew that attraction could make people do funny things—and really stupid things, too—he didn't think that was it, not completely. Dane had shown more care for him than anyone had in years.

Not since my mom died.

When Danny had reached the door, he hadn't been able to touch it. The words Dane had rumbled in his soothing bass had echoed through his body in an almost physical way. The man wanted to love and cherish him.

Why am I walking away from that? Even if he can turn into a giant lizard—komodo dragon. Whatever.

Turning back around, Danny had asked the only thing that he couldn't seem to get his mind around. "Why me?"

Dane's full lips curved into a small smile. His dark eyes warmed. Even his handsome features appeared to soften.

"Why not you, Danny?" Dane countered. "You're obviously hardworking. Kind and forgiving." His nostrils flared as his attention dropped to Danny's cast for an instant before meeting his gaze once more. "Long-suffering and patient. Being bonded with a man like you would be a dream come true." With a grimace, Dane added, "How do you know you're not getting the short end of the stick? I can be dominant, impetuous, and overbearing. I told you I'm old, and I'm stuck in my ways. I've had a hard life, and sometimes it makes me cold and thoughtless." He let out a deep breath before finishing, "With you, I want to be better. You make me better just by being with you."

Nothing in Dane's behavior had seemed like that to Danny—*Well, okay. Maybe the dominant and impetuous part.* No way would Danny have thought he would have a hook-up at work.

Taking a step back toward the bed, then another, Danny tried to recall everything Dane and Dakota had spouted—Fates and soul mates and paranormals . . . bonding.

There was so much, and Danny guessed that what they'd

shared was really only the tip of the iceberg.

"So, you mentioned Fates." Danny rested his good hand on the rumpled comforter. "They pair you with someone." Something tripped through his brain. "Does that mean you don't decide?"

"Not in the way you're thinking," Dane countered, shaking his head. "I—"

Danny made the mistake of resting his injured hand on the bed, and a throb immediately started up his limb, causing him to wince and jerk his hand back up. The sudden movement didn't help. His head swam a little as black spots flashed across his vision.

"Danny?" Solid hands rested on Danny's shoulders, massaging lightly. "Shit, honey. You shouldn't be up. Please lie down." The hands encouraged him to turn and relax. "Let's elevate that wrist. Would an icepack help? Do you have any painkillers? I can call Dakota and have him find some for you."

Allowing Dane to position him back onto the bed, Danny focused on breathing and getting the pulsing waves of agony rippling up his limb to ebb. "Pain meds in my pocket," he admitted roughly. "Crap. Put pressure on it, and I shouldna."

Feeling Dane reach into first one pocket, then the other, should have been sexy . . . if sweat hadn't popped out on his brow.

"Lie still," Dane ordered. "I'll get you water to take this."

As if I can go anywhere with my head swimming.

Danny vaguely noticed the sound of running water. Then Dane was back at his side.

"Open."

When Danny obeyed, Dane placed a pill on his tongue. He cradled Danny's head in one large hand, tilting his face up a smidge. Danny felt the rim of a glass against his bottom lip.

"Drink."

Once more, Danny did as he was told.

Dane carefully trickled water into Danny's mouth, allowing him to swallow the pill.

"Okay. I'm going to lift your wrist and slide a pillow under it," Dane continued, his voice low and soothing. "We'll get this elevated a bit. I hear that's good for a broken limb."

After a small nod from Danny, Dane put word to deed. A second later, Dane eased away, and Danny watched him through slitted eyelids. He spotted the big man heading back into the bathroom, and water ran again. When he returned, Dane carried a damp cloth.

Dane climbed into bed and stretched out beside him. Resting his weight on his forearm, the sexy man gently ran the cool cloth over Danny's forehead, clearing away the sweat.

"I'm sorry I scared you enough to try to run, Danny." A hint of pain laced Dane's tone and words. "That was never my intention. I never wanted you afraid of me. You're my everything."

Danny sighed and relaxed, enjoying Dane's gentle ministrations. After a few minutes of quiet, he heard Dane ask, "How do you feel now? Better?"

Dipping his chin in a small nod, Danny admitted, "Although I think I missed most of your explanation." Danny couldn't even remember noticing when Dane had moved off the bed.

"Do you want me to try to repeat it?"

Do I?

With Dane there at his side, tending to him gently, Danny tried to figure out why the reason mattered. It didn't. Even if Dane was only there because the Fates decided they were perfect for each other, what did it matter?

"No," Danny murmured. He turned his head a little to focus on Dane's concerned features. "I don't think I care why some mythical gods decided we're perfect together."

Dane chuckled softly. "They're not so mythical, my mate, but I understand most humans don't believe in them these days." With a wry smile, he added, "So many people get so wrapped up in technology and careers and the pursuit of money and stuff that they lose sight of what's really important."

Danny arched one brow. "What's that?"

"Spending time with family and friends," Dane answered quietly. "Forging bonds of love with those we care about."

Sadness welled up in Danny. "I don't have family or friends to forge anything with."

Dane's grunt sounded almost wounded. He swallowed so hard his Adam's apple bobbed. Leaning close, he whispered into Danny's ear, "You do now, if you'll allow it."

Danny turned his head, catching Dane's gaze. "What do you mean?" His attention dipped a little. Dane's lips were so close.

"I mean me, Dakota, my brother Del and his mate Miggs." Dane closed the distance between them, pressing a chaste kiss to the corner of Danny's mouth. "We'd be your family and friends." Drawing back a little, Dane smirked. "Of course, that means you'll have to put up with Dakota's foot-in-mouth syndrome, and I know you haven't met him yet, but Del can be gruff and a bit of a bastard, but he raised us after our parents died, so he had to grow up damn fast."

"I'm sorry," Danny whispered. He knew all about the loss of a beloved parent.

Dane shook his head. "It was a long, *long* time ago." Setting the washcloth aside, he teased his fingers through Danny's hair, rubbing a lock between his fingers. Dane wasn't looking at him when he asked, "Will you tell you why you tried to take off?"

Sighing, Danny thought about that. Maybe it was the pain meds loosening his tongue, but he admitted, "I freaked out. Panicked. You'd told me that you turn into . . . well, practically a dinosaur, just like your brother did." Narrowing his eyes, Danny stared at the ceiling. He sank into Dane's gentle touches to his scalp as he fondled his hair. "That stuff isn't supposed to happen in real life. I was never into fantasy, and that's straight out of . . . I don't even know."

Danny cut his gaze to Dane, finding the other man's intense gaze upon him. "It's a little hard to wrap my brain around the fact that I'm lying next to a guy who turns into a lizard." Sweeping his focus down Dane's frame, he felt saliva pool in his mouth as he admired Dane's broad torso and thickly defined muscles. "You're so damn sexy, but you're not human. How is this even possible?" Furrowing his brows, Danny whispered, "I'd blame it on the pain meds, but I don't have this kind of imagination." He knew it was grossly inappropriate, but even confused and still in a bit of pain, his prick took notice of the handsome man lying next to him, thickening in his jeans. "I've never done anything with anyone, and yet, I want to let you do everything to me."

Groaning, Dane pressed his temple against Danny's. "Gods, my mate," he mumbled. "The things you tempt me to do, but I can't." Mouthing kisses along Danny's jaw, Dane repeated, "I want to worship every inch of your body with my tongue, open up your pretty virgin hole, and sink my cock deep inside you. I want to spill in you, bite you, and bond us for eternity." Dane's warm breath danced across Danny's skin, causing goose bumps to erupt on his neck, before Dane continued, "But I fear I'd hurt your arm, and hurting you in any way would absolutely gut me." Then Dane moaned his name softly before whispering, "But gods, you smell so good."

Tipping his head to the side, Danny let out a groan of his own. His dick throbbed just listening to Dane's words. His body flushed hot as his blood rushed through his veins. He even felt his balls ache.

Feeling Dane working his mouth down the side of his jaw,

Danny panted softly. The hairs on his neck stood on end. The sensation trickled down his arms and across his chest, causing his nipples to bead. His gut clenched as his dick twitched behind his fly, leaking pre-cum.

Danny recalled the feel of Dane's hand on his erection in the bathroom, and a fresh wash of need surged through him. It had felt so good — this man's touch. He desperately wanted to feel that again, but he wasn't certain how to make it happen.

Perhaps . . .

"Please, Dane," Danny muttered. "I . . . I—"

"Anything, my mate," Dane crooned between suckling kisses to his neck and throat. "Say it, and it's yours."

"T-Touch me."

Dane chuckled huskily, the warmth of his breath sending a fresh wave of heat across his skin. "I am touching you."

With his arousal making him feel bold, Danny grabbed Dane's wrist. He tugged the man's hand from his hair and brought it down . . . down where he needed to feel it more than his next breath. The first press of Dane's palm against his erection yanked a barked cry from between his lips.

Once Dane's hand was cupping Danny's cloth-covered dick, he needed no further encouragement. He massaged Danny's length through the denim. His strong hand squeezed and relaxed, creating the most exquisite of sensations.

"This what you need, Danny?" Dane asked, his voice deep and gruff, betraying his own lust. "You need me to touch your length, my mate?"

"Yessss," Danny hissed, bucking his hips, pressing harder into the man's hold.

"Easy, honey," Dane rumbled. "Don't jostle your arm."

Danny didn't know if that was possible, especially upon feeling Dane making quick work of his fly.

"Gonna have to show you the joys of going commando," Dane grumbled as he eased the flaps aside. "Lift your hips a bit. Let's give your lovely cock more room."

While Danny wondered if he should feel embarrassed, he did as he was told. Planting his feet, he lifted his hips. Dane quickly yanked not only his jeans but his underwear partway down his thighs, exposing his cock and balls. Danny's erection swung up, slapping his stomach, sending tingles through his shaft that went straight to his balls.

Before Danny could utter a word, Dane gripped his length in a tight, sure hold and began a slow jacking.

"I dreamed of touching you again every night," Dane purred, holding Danny's gaze with his own heated one. "The feel of your silky length in my palm, the scent of your arousal perfuming the air, and the sound of your whimpers as you revel in my touch." His voice dropped to a low guttural rumble. "It all sets my blood on fire. I love seeing your responses, so pure, so perfect." Dane's smile turned feral. "Did you know I came with barely a touch in the bathroom the other day? All I needed was the taste of your seed, the scent of your need. It caused my balls to ache in the best possible way."

Gasping in surprise, Danny trembled. "R-Really?"

"Mmm-hmmm," Dane confirmed. Returning his mouth to Danny's jaw, he muttered, "You're perfect, mate of mine. Oh, so perfect."

Danny had never had anyone call him perfect before. If they had, he wouldn't have believed them anyway. But as Dane played with his erection, mouthed kisses on his neck and jaw, and rumbled words of devotion, he could almost believe.

"Perfect," Dane insisted, tightening his grip on Danny's length just a bit more.

The way Dane swiped his thumb over Danny's crown, dipping his nail lightly into the slit in the process, was the final straw, sending his orgasm crashing through him and his senses soaring as he screamed Dane's name.

CHAPTER EIGHT

Dane's cock throbbed behind the confines of his fly, but he resisted the urge to rut against Danny's hip. When his mate had asked for what he needed, pride had burst through Dane, and not a little bit of satisfaction. Danny was coming to trust him.

Plus, as he was pleasuring Danny, it occurred to Dane that an orgasm was nature's natural painkiller.

Gently petting Danny's spent erection, Dane swept his gaze over his mate's flushed face and panting body. He'd made a mess out of his lover's shirt, but he'd get him a new one. Hell, he needed to get his mate a whole slew of things.

Gotta get him to accept our bond first.

Hearing Danny's breathing even out, Dane returned his attention to his mate's face. Seeing the relaxed features there, he smiled. His mate had passed right back out again.

Dane guessed it was caused by a number of things. His body was healing, meaning he needed more sleep. His mind was processing with a whole load of crap—from losing his home, job, being beaten by his father, to learning about shifters. Then, of course, he'd taken some painkillers, which often made humans sleepy.

As Dane eased away from his sleeping mate, he smiled. Danny had stayed. He'd allowed Dane to care for him. Even if it was mostly due to his injury, Dane would take it. It meant their connection was growing, strengthening.

Once Dane was off the bed, he adjusted his erection before

heading to the coffee table. He picked up his phone and noticed two missed texts. Opening the first, he smiled.

It was from Miggs. *Del just told me you found your mate. Congrats! Can't wait to meet him.*

Dane chuckled softly. When he'd first found out that Fate had paired his hard-assed council interrogator brother with a sweet guinea pig shifter, he'd wondered what the hell they were thinking. After seeing them together, though, Dane had understood. Del had needed a little lightness, a little joy, in his life, and Miggs had needed a protector.

They were perfect for each other.

The second message was from Dakota. *Hope Danny's okay. Everything all right? Didn't mean to botch shit up for you.*

Pressing a button to dial Dakota, Dane moved back to the bed. He picked up the discarded washcloth and returned to the bathroom. He'd just turned on the water when his brother picked up, sounding groggy.

"Yeah. Everyone okay?"

Shit. What time is it?

"Hey, Kota," Dane greeted softly, tucking his phone between his ear and shoulder. "Didn't mean to wake you. The curtains are all drawn in here, and I didn't check the clock."

"It's alright," Dakota drawled around a yawn. "It's, um, just after five."

That made sense. Danny was used to rising early.

"Damn. Sorry again."

The sound of scratching came through the line, and Dane wasn't certain he wanted to guess at what Dakota was doing. After ringing out the wet cloth, he headed back to the bedroom to clean up his mate.

Dakota grunted, then the unmistakable sound of someone urinating filled Dane's ear.

Dane rolled his eyes, but he didn't comment on it. As he cleaned Dane, he quietly shared what had happened — minus giving his mate a hand job. He just left it at him holding

Danny and helping him relax. Still, Dakota chortled, so Dane figured his brother was making some educated guesses. Ignoring that, Dane once again removed his mate's shoes and socks, taking his jeans with them. Then he carefully pulled his underwear back up before tucking him back into bed.

As Dane did that, he continued to talk to Dakota. "I'm hoping that I can talk him into moving in with me," Dane admitted, ever the optimist. "There's nothing for him here."

"Do you really think he'll agree?"

Ignoring the doubt in Dakota's voice, Dane told his brother, "If we show him support, I think so. Give him options, anyway, even if it's offering an apartment near our homes." Dane needed Danny living close to him so damn badly. Before his brother could reply, he quickly added, "Do you think you could scrounge up some boxes? I'd like to take him back to his old home and help him gather anything he wants to take with him."

"Boxes?" Dakota sounded doubtful. "We're on motorcycles. How do you expect to carry them?"

Dane rolled his eyes as he eased onto the sofa and relaxed. "We can ship them from the post office."

"Oh, yeah. Of course." Dakota sounded a little more with it, and Dane wondered if his brother had made a cup of coffee.

He thought about doing the same but worried the scent would wake Danny. Hopefully, his mate would sleep a bit longer while he put his plans in motion. Plus, Dane hoped his human woke calmer than the last time, too.

"I'll look up nearest grocery stores and such and make a few calls," Dakota assured him. Yep, that time Dane definitely heard him sipping something. "Then grab some bungees, too. We can strap the empty ones to the back of your bike for the ride over there."

Dane nodded absently. "I noticed a diner down the road. We can meet there for breakfast in say . . . two hours?"

Dakota chuckled. "That gonna be enough time for you to convince your cutie to bond with you?"

At the mention of bonding, Dane's animal rumbled in his mind. His mouth watered, and he totally agreed with his dragon. He wanted to seal the deal with his love in the worst way.

Patience, he reminded his animal.

"I'm not going to push that, yet," Dane replied. "We'll get there."

"He'd heal faster if you claimed him."

Dane hummed, knowing his brother was right. He just didn't think that was a good reason for them to join their lives. Call him a romantic, but Dane wanted Danny to accept him as a person, not because of the many benefits humans gained by accepting their paranormal mate.

"Well, I'll do researchin'," Dakota promised him.

"Thanks, Kota." Dane began to pull the phone from his ear before returning it and quickly adding, "And, Dakota?"

"Yeah?"

"You didn't screw up anything with me and Danny. We'll get there." Then Dane chuckled softly, saying, "Although you'd better pray that your mate is a paranormal."

Dakota groaned. "I know, right?"

After another quiet laugh, Dane said, "See you soon," and disconnected the call.

When Dane lowered the phone, his attention once again strayed to Danny. To his surprise, he saw his mate's eyes were open, and he was staring at him. Dane smiled, pleased to get a smile in return.

"It's early, yet," Dane murmured. "Do you want to try sleeping a bit longer?"

Danny opened his mouth, hesitated, and closed it.

Dane waited patiently and was rewarded.

"Will you hold me?"

At the whispered words, Dane quickly rose from the sofa. He crossed to the bed, placed the phone on the nightstand, and reached for the fly of his jeans. They were getting uncomfortable, but he wasn't certain if Danny was ready for nudity.

Lowering his hands, Dane made a move to climb in still clothed.

Danny touched his wrist. "You can take those off . . . i-if you want to."

Dane sucked in a surprised breath as he roved his gaze over Danny's face, searching. He noticed how his mate nibbled his bottom lip and how his cheeks were a bit flushed. Still, Danny continued to hold Dane's focus.

Taking that as a win, Dane unzipped his jeans. His erection, which hadn't softened much, even on his call, instantly separated the flaps. Dane heard Danny's inhalation, but he didn't make a big deal of it.

Instead, Dane quickly shucked his dirty jeans before crawling into bed beside Danny. He curved his bigger body around his smaller mate's side. His human was still clothed in his shirt and underwear, but he could still feel the heat of his lover's skin through the thin fabric, and it felt glorious.

Settling his head on the pillow beside Danny's, Dane curled his arm around his mate's waist as he slung his leg over the man's thighs. He held him close, relaxing, just breathing in his scent. His erection rested against Danny's cloth-covered hip, and he did his best to ignore it.

Holding his mate was enough for now.

"How are you feeling?" Dane asked softly, rubbing his fingertips over Danny's shirt-covered side. "Your arm settled a little?"

Danny squinted as if thinking deeply before he answered. "Just a dull ache. If I don't move it much, it's fine."

Appreciating Danny's honesty, Dane murmured, "We're

to have breakfast at the diner in a couple of hours with Dakota. We can use the plastic bag meant for the ice bucket to keep your cast dry if you want to shower in a bit." Dane had noticed it the evening before.

"That would be nice," Danny replied, although his gaze strayed to the hot tub. "How long are we staying here?"

Dane loved his mate's use of the word *we*.

"We can stay for a while, if you like," Dane told him. "I have at least a two-week leave." Seeing Danny's brows shoot up, he added, "That's standard for when a shifter finds his mate in a human. Sometimes, it can take a while to woo them."

Scoffing, Danny muttered, "Woo."

"Mmm-hmmm," Dane confirmed. Leaning forward, he couldn't resist bussing his lips across Danny's temple. "Every mate is a gift from Fate," he reminded. "They deserve to be courted and cared for."

For a long moment, Danny didn't reply. Finally, he met Dane's gaze. "I like that."

"Me, too."

That time, Dane pressed a kiss to Danny's lips in a light touch. When his mate opened easily to him, he couldn't resist a deeper taste. Sliding his tongue into his human's mouth, he lapped gently, reacquainting himself with Danny's taste.

So damn good.

Dane eased back, knowing if he didn't stop, it would instantly go to his head. Plus, he was already damn near suffering a case of blue balls. If he did much more, he would end up rutting all over Danny and soiling his shirt.

Damn it. I really need to find my mate some clothes before breakfast.

Except, the feel of soft fingers tentatively stroking over his cock head drove the thought out of his mind. His erection flexed, and he gasped. Instinctively, he pushed forward and was rewarded with a firmer touch—Danny skating his fingertips over his crown and under the flared head.

"Oh, gods, Danny." Dane couldn't remember a time when so little stimulation caused such a riot in his bloodstream. "Mate."

Danny must have taken that for the permission it was. He turned his body toward him a bit, allowing him better access while keeping his injured hand tight to his chest and out of the way. Wrapping his fingers around Dane's erection, just under the head, he squeezed tightly while flicking his thumb over and around the crown before massaging the sensitive bundle underneath.

Groaning, Dane lifted his right knee, planting that foot. He opened himself to Danny's explorations, wishing he could shove the blanket aside so he could watch his mate's first explorations. Instead, Dane held Danny's gaze, hoping to encourage him with his expression.

It seemed to work.

Slowly, Danny began jacking his length, alternating the pressure. He massaged his nerve bundle and teased at his crown. When he reached farther and cupped his balls, Dane rocked into the hold and groaned his mate's name.

Realizing that was a hot spot for him, Danny squeezed lightly before gently massaging his testicles.

Dane's erection jerked and twitched. His balls began to tighten. The tingle at the base of his spine told him it'd been far too long and he was about to lose his load so damn fast.

"Danny," Dane rumbled, panting. "Oh, gods. Please don't stop."

"Wanna see you come," Danny whispered. "Like the way you feel, tense and trembling under my fingers."

Groaning, Dane managed to pant, "You keep doing that. Ugh." He had to suck in another lungful of air before finishing, "And I'll blow damn fast."

If anything, Danny managed to speed up his movements. He massaged Dane's orbs for another few seconds before returning his focus to his shaft. He squeezed, stroked, teased, and tortured.

When Dane's balls pulled up and his release hit him, he opened his mouth and let out a long, low moan. His cock pulsed, and his endorphins sent his senses floating. Bliss coated his mind, the sensations extended by Danny continuing to pet his twitching erection. Finally, Dane began to soften, and Danny eased his hold, although he continued to tease his fingertips over his flesh.

Swallowing hard, twice, Dane opened eyes he couldn't remember closing. He smiled, taking in Danny's look of awe. His mate's smile appeared to be one of wonder, as if he couldn't figure out how he could offer Dane such pleasure.

If only he knew.

Dane decided to tell him. "Oh, Danny," he murmured, leaning forward to share a long, languorous kiss. Smiling, he rested his face on his mate's pillow, their faces just a few inches apart. "Your touch is the most exquisite thing I've ever experienced." Dane still felt pinging aftershocks. "Thank you so very much."

"That was good then?" Danny whispered, obviously uncertain.

"*More* than good," Dane assured. "Mind-bending, my mate." Letting out a rough chuckle, he added, "If just your hand on me feels like that, actual sex and claiming is going to send me into orbit."

Danny snickered. "Claiming?" he asked, tipping his head a little. "What's that?"

Right. Still so much to explain.

Humming, Dane explained, "Claiming is how a shifter bonds with his mate, twining their life-threads, so they can remain together for the rest of their lives." Reaching up, he touched the side of Danny's neck that was already covered in pale red marks because he couldn't resist working that bit of flesh. "I'll bite you here." Upon seeing Danny's shocked look, and guessing at what his sweet human was thinking, he waggled his brows and told him, "It will make you orgasm. You'll love it."

Clearly disbelieving, Danny questioned, "I'll orgasm from your bite? How's that work?" He frowned. "Doesn't biting usually hurt?"

"Not in this case." Dane shrugged one shoulder. "And don't ask me how it works. It just does. Must be a paranormal thing so mates aren't afraid to be claimed."

While Danny still appeared a bit uncertain, he still nodded. "So, um, claiming is like marriage."

Dane nodded. "Yes, except without divorce." He spotted the way Danny's brows shot up, so he quickly added, "I'll never stray, my mate. You are my world, and I'll always put your needs first. Your safety and happiness." Growling softly, Dane rubbed up and down Danny's arm, adding, "And we're possessive bastards, so I hope you'll be okay with some PDA."

"O-Okay." After nibbling his bottom lip for a few seconds, Danny shifted restlessly. Suddenly, pink bloomed in his cheeks. "I, uh, I think I got some of your, uh, your stuff on my clothes."

For a second, Dane's orgasm-addled brain didn't follow. Once he did, he whipped back the covers. "Oh," he murmured, seeing that Danny's shirt and even his underwear had both become victims to his spray.

Although, as Dane helped his blushing mate peel off his clothes, cover his cast, and get into the shower, he and his animal preened that even a thorough washing wouldn't remove their scent from their mate.

CHAPTER NINE

Danny stared at himself in the mirror. He couldn't remember the last time he'd worn clothes so nice. His blue jeans were designer, as was his green polo shirt. Even the boots on his feet were more expensive than any three pairs he'd ever bought combined.

In a word, he looked . . . amazing.

He finally understood the expression *the man makes the clothes.*

"Hey, does everything fit okay?" Dane knocked gently on the bathroom door. "Can I see?"

After inhaling deeply, Danny let out slowly. "Come in." He wished his voice could have come out stronger.

Dane opened the door. As he looked him up and down, a warm smile creased his lips. "Dakota does have excellent fashion sense." With a wink, Dane reached for his left hand and tugged him forward. "It must be to make up for his big mouth."

"Hey, I resemble that remark," Dakota called, laughter in his tone. As soon as Danny cleared the doorway, the brother let out a wolf whistle. "Very nice, Danny." He blew on his fingertips, then rubbed them on his shirt as if buffing them. "If I do say so myself."

Laughing, Dane picked up an empty paper coffee cup and chucked it at him. "Get your own damn mate to ogle."

Easily dodging the container, Dakota grinned broadly. "Hey, it's not my fault you asked me to snag something for Danny since I was already out and about." Then he sobered and added, "And I'm definitely trying, bro. You have no idea."

Dane reached over and gripped Dakota's shoulder in what could only be called brotherly support. "You'll find him or her, Kota. Patience."

Blowing out a breath, Dakota smiled. "Yeah, not sure it's my virtue, though." He moved away from them both, starting toward the door. "All joking aside, though, Danny." He paused and turned, giving him two thumbs up. "You look fantastic. Hope you don't have a problem with the style."

"Oh, I don't mind at all," Danny quickly assured with a shake of his head. Looking down at himself, he stated, "These are wonderful, but"—he again focused on Dakota—"I have no idea how I'll ever pay your back."

Dakota blew a raspberry while rolling his eyes. "Pay me back? Ha." Shaking his head, he grinned at him. "You're my brother's mate. That makes you family. You don't pay back family." With another laugh, Dakota grabbed the door handle. "Besides, it's family money, so it's yours anyway."

Then Dakota disappeared out the door.

As Dane helped him into the leather jacket from yesterday, Danny asked, "What's that mean? Family money?"

"Hmm?" Dane glanced up from where he was bringing the zipper up a third of the way. "Oh, my brothers and I pool our money. Always have. Family money." With an arm around Danny's shoulders, Dane guided them out. "With us all being almost two hundred years old, we've had quite some time to build up a nest egg." He winked. "We're rich enough where you'd never have to work another day in your life if you didn't want to. We work for the council because we're all big dominants and would end up bored to tears within a week."

Holy shit. These guys are rich?

Danny didn't know how to respond to that.

As they walked out the door, Dane holding it for him, the big man dipped his head and stated, "Please don't let that put you off. Money is just a tool."

Even as Danny nodded, he would guess that was just because the guy never had a lack of it.

Wait. That's uncharitable. How do I know if Dane has ever been poor? He was born almost two hundred years ago. Like he said, that was a lot of time to learn how to earn money and make it grow.

When Danny spotted the metallic purple bullet bike resting next to Dane's, he shook his head. "No way I'm getting on that," he whispered.

Dakota grinned broadly. "Aww, cutie. You wound me." He rested his hands over his heart dramatically. "I'd never let anything happen to you."

Dane growled as he unlocked the back of the *Harley.* "Don't worry, honey," he murmured. "I'm not a speed demon like my brother." Placing the helmet he retrieved on Danny's head, he buckled it while saying, "I like to cruise and relax. I don't own one of those."

Relief flooded Danny. "Good."

Dakota laughed again, the sound becoming muffled as he flipped down his helmet's visor.

Shaking his head, Dane helped Danny onto the bike. "We're just zipping around to the diner," he stated, fastening his own helmet. "I'm looking forward to breakfast."

At the mention of food, Danny's stomach rumbled in agreement.

"What are the empty boxes bungeed to your bike for?" Danny asked, glancing out the front window as he sipped his hot chocolate.

They were just finishing their morning meals and drinks when Danny finally voiced the question nagging at him.

Dakota froze with his coffee cup halfway to his lips. "You didn't ask yet?" He stared incredulously at Dane.

Dane chewed and swallowed his bite of sausage, then cleared his throat. His expression turned a little sheepish as he admitted, "I, uh . . . got distracted." Focusing on Danny, Dane gave him a wry smile. "You're really distracting, honey."

Confused—and a little pleased his huge, sexy blond lover found him so distracting—Danny pressed, "Sooo . . . what do you need to ask me?"

Setting down his fork, Dane reached over and placed his palm on Danny's left wrist. The big man had been honest. He didn't have one problem with public displays of affection. Dane had touched his wrist, held his fingers, and placed his hand on Danny's thigh more times than he could count throughout breakfast.

He found he liked it very much.

"So, you said you fled your home with only the shirt on your back," Dane began softly, his tone making it obvious that he was trying not to upset Danny by bringing up the painful subject. After Danny had nodded, Dane told him, "I was thinking that, maybe, you'd left behind a few important things, and you'd like to claim them." Dane glanced Dakota's way before focusing on him again. "My brother and I will keep you safe the entire time you're there. That's what the boxes are for."

"Oh." Danny breathed the word. Huh. "That's actually . . . very thoughtful of you." Frowning, he added, "But I have no-where to put anything."

"Well, I was hoping you would consider letting us mail it, uh . . . to my place."

Danny took in Dane's hopeful expression. "Your place?"

Dane nodded. "I've explained our instincts to you," he re-plied, lowering his voice as he leaned closer. "I would really—" He hesitated, his expression turning strained. After a second frowning at the table, Dane met his gaze again. "Leaving you the first time was the hardest damn thing I've ever had to do. I don't want to do that again. I want you with me." Lifting his free hand as if to stop Danny from speaking—as if he had any response to that anyway—Dane quickly added, "If you're not comfortable living with me yet, then we'll find an apartment or condo for you to rent for the time being. Just . . . something in Savannah. Close to me."

"Oh," Danny whispered, understanding. "Y-You're, uh, you're asking me to move in with you . . . after just a few days."

Dakota reached over and patted him on the shoulder. "We do things fast, sure, but you know it's right."

Danny opened his mouth, preparing to question Dakota's statement. Then he snapped his mouth shut.

Huh. It does feel right.

Any time Danny was with Dane, it felt right. He was about to wonder what that meant, but seeing the expectant, hopeful look on Dane's face and the smiling one on Dakota's—who continued to eat his biscuits and gravy as if nothing unusual was taking place. Maybe that was it. For a shifter, there was nothing unusual taking place.

Shifters found their fated mate, bonded, and built a life together.

So that's what he's been trying to explain all this time.

It was only humans who would think it odd, since most didn't believe in love at first sight. Plus, technically, they didn't say it was love at first sight, either. They said they recognized someone they could build a life with, but it was still work.

When Dane had left, Danny had missed him so badly. Every time he'd received a text, his heart would race wildly. Their phone calls had been the highlight of his days. Lying in Dane's arms, whether they were talking or doing more, had been the best moments of Danny's life.

Why the hell shouldn't he grab onto that with both hands and never let go?

Just when uncertainty and worry clouded Dane's face,

Danny grinned. "I would very much love to move in with you."

While Dane grabbed Danny and hauled him onto his lap, hugging him close and capturing his lips, Dakota jumped from his chair with a whoop.

The noise must have drawn plenty of attention, but all Danny could think about was the feel of Dane's lips against his own. He wasn't a fan of coffee, but he could get used to it second hand on his lover's tongue. There was no way he'd give up kissing his man for any reason.

"Is everything okay?"

Danny recognized the waitress's voice, and Dane must have, too. He broke the kiss and helped ease Danny back onto his own chair, but he pulled it closer to his side. Dane even rested his arm across the back, a wide grin splitting his face.

It was Dakota who answered.

With a huge grin on his face too, Dakota claimed, "My brother's boyfriend just agreed to marry him."

Danny felt his face go up in flames. He opened his mouth, then closed it again. While that hadn't really been what happened, he supposed it was close enough to the truth. After all, living with a shifter meant claiming, right?

"U-Um, con-congratulations?" the flustered waitress stuttered. Her face was red, and she couldn't seem to meet any of their gazes. "I-Is there, um, a-anything I can g-get you?"

"Yes," Dane answered. "Your largest cinnamon roll with extra icing, if possible." Winking at Danny, he added, "We're celebrating."

"Of course," the waitress replied before rushing away.

Danny noticed a few of the customers scowling at him, but even more people were smiling, obviously happy for them.

Huh.

After their impromptu celebration, Danny found himself back on the back of Dane's bike returning to his hometown.

He felt the nerves skittering through him, and he did his best to breathe. Fear of meeting his father kept him from enjoying the ride.

When they reached Danny's house, he saw his father's car in the driveway. That wasn't really a surprise, considering the man didn't work. He lived off his mother's life insurance policy.

It was a good thing the house had been paid for, or his father would have lost it years before.

"Okay," Dakota announced as he swung off his bike and pulled his helmet from his head in one fluid motion. A grin lit his blond features. "Let's do this."

In Danny's opinion, Dakota looked way too excited.

Dane chuckled as he eased off the bike. As he helped Danny dismount and remove his helmet, he quietly told him, "Dakota loves putting assholes in their place, regardless of the type of asshole."

As Danny watched Dane unclasp the boxes from the back of the bike, he removed his jacket. Dakota was there in an instant to take it and fold it into one of the other saddlebags. While scratching at the skin at the top of his cast, Danny peered at the quiet house and nibbled his bottom lip.

"You ready to do this, honey?" Dane asked, wrapping his free arm around Danny's shoulders.

"Guys, please don't hurt my father," Danny murmured, uncertainty flooding him. "Maybe this isn't such a good idea."

"We won't harm him," Dakota assured, his expression sobering to one of understanding. "But if he goes after you, we will defend you. You're my brother's mate. You're family."

When Danny peered at Dane, his lover nodded.

After another breath to gird up his courage, Danny nodded. "Okay." After all, there were a few mementos from his mother that he'd hated leaving behind.

Sure hope he hasn't trashed my room, yet.

Pulling his keys from his pocket, Danny made his way up the walk. He slid the key home and unlocked the door. Then he entered.

Danny had made it through the foyer and halfway to the hall when his father appeared through a doorway on the right — the living room. He froze, as if he were a deer in headlights.

"There you are. Bout time you showed up," his father growled with a curl of his lip. Holding out his hand, he ordered, "Tip money. Now. I need to go buy beer."

What the hell?

"I-I—" Danny didn't know what to say. "I don't—"

"What do you mean you *don't*?" His father stalked toward him. "I want money. I—" He frowned, finally spotting Dane and Dakota, although, how he'd missed them in the first place, Danny had no idea. Glaring at the pair, his father demanded, "Who the fuck are you guys? Get out of my house."

Did his father not remember two nights ago? Breaking his arm and running him from the house?

While Danny couldn't seem to find his tongue, Dane had no such trouble. "We'll leave as soon as we help Danny gather his belongings."

"What the hell are you talking about?" His father narrowed his eyes as he looked over the trio. Finally, his hard gaze settled on Danny. "You ain't goin' nowhere, boy. I own your ass, and you'll do as you're told."

"Danny is a legal adult, and if he wishes to move out, he can." Dane started urging him forward again. "Besides, just yesterday morning, you told me he didn't live here anymore."

"I've never seen you before in my life," his father claimed. "If you don't get out of here, I'm callin' the police."

Dakota snorted. "Oh, please do, Mister Nunez. Please do."

With his father engaged with Dakota, Danny hurried down the hall to his bedroom. To his shock, when he pushed open the door, he found that the room hadn't been touched. His bed was still neatly made, his school books were still on the shelves, and everything was neat as a pin.

"There's something a bit off about your father," Dane whispered into his ear. "Where do you want me to start?"

Danny was getting that same distinct impression. "The closet."

As Dane set up a box, using packing tape to hold it in place, Danny opened the closet door and tried to ignore the fact that his father had, indeed, decided to call the cops.

CHAPTER TEN

"It's nice to meet you," Danny offered nervously, holding out his left hand.

Del took Danny's left hand with his own left, offering him a gentle shake. "I'm very glad to meet you, Danny," the huge man offered, although he didn't really smile. "I'm very happy for you and Dane. He's a good guy. He'll take care of you."

Danny glanced around at the brothers, struggling with how to respond. "Um, thanks. I-I hope to be able to take care of him, too."

Dane grinned, squeezing Danny's shoulder since he still had his arm around him. "Just being with you is enough," he murmured into Danny's hair. Then he pointed at the diminutive man crushed to Del's side. "And this is Del's mate, Miggs."

To Danny's surprise, Miggs tore from Del's grip and wrapped him in a hug, taking care not to squish Danny's wrist. "It's so nice to meet you. I'm so happy for you both." He grinned broadly at him, easing back a step and resting his hands on Danny's upper arms. Really, the guy couldn't have stood more than five-foot-one and made Danny feel large. "So, we should go sightseeing. There are so many—Eep!"

Del grabbed Miggs around the waist and yanked him back into his arms, causing Miggs to erupt into a round of laughter. The small man grinned up at Del, love shining in his eyes. The heavily-built man's icy expression melted as he smiled at Miggs, completely transforming his face.

Wow!

"Yes, my brother's damn possessive of who his mate touches," Dakota stated with a laugh, shouldering past them toward the ice chest. "Want a beer, Danny, or are you on meds where you can't have them?"

"He's not mated, yet," Del grumbled, as if that explained his actions. "Once my brother claims Danny, then you can hug him, Miggs."

Miggs smiled fondly at Del. "Yes, my mate. I know you're a jealous bastard for no reason. It's just . . . even without a mark, he's still family."

Del nodded once. "Yes, he is, but I'm still a jealous bastard."

Miggs just laughed.

"Um, no thanks," Danny replied, focusing on Dakota's question instead. "I'll just have a *Sprite* or lemonade, if you have it."

Dakota gave him a thumbs up and bent to rummage through the cooler.

Danny had been living with Dane for three days already. While he wanted Dane in that way, Dane had never broached the subject, even on the drive south. They'd returned to the hotel for a second night and enjoyed the suite's *Jacuzzi* tub together. They'd rubbed off together but nothing more.

Now that Danny felt a little more settled, Dane had taken him to his brother Dakota's home for a small barbeque. Small was a relative word. Dane had introduced him to over a dozen people, and there were still people he hadn't met.

Fortunately, everyone was friendly, making him feel welcome.

"Hey, Danny," Theo greeted. The man was also a human, who was mated with a grizzly bear shifter. "Try these."

Danny eyed the plate Theo was holding up. It looked like a peanut butter bar topped with chocolate. Picking up one, he took a small bite.

Groaning as wonderful flavors burst across his tongue, Danny quickly took a larger bite. He closed his eyes and savored the delicious treat.

"I love the sounds you're making," Dane whispered into his ear with a growl. "I'd *love* to hear them in another setting."

Sucking in a surprised breath, Danny nearly choked on the bite of food he'd been enjoying. He quickly swallowed as he shifted his stance. His dick had become so hard so fast, he was nearly lightheaded.

Oh, wow.

Peering up at Dane, Danny saw the way his lover's eyes were narrowed. He had a definite predatory look gleaming in his eyes. Even his nostrils were flared.

Danny took in that expression and a feeling of boldness surged through him. "Wh-What did you have in mind?"

Dane growled under his breath as he nuzzled his temple with his nose. "You're playing with fire, honey. I've been trying so very hard to be good."

"What do you mean?" Danny whispered, confused.

"To take care of you, woo you, like you deserve," Dane replied gruffly. "But doing things like that . . . you make it so difficult."

"Wait," Theo cut in, a crease furrowing his brows. He pointed between them. "You haven't claimed Danny, yet?" He frowned. "Why the hell not?"

"Theo, love," Theo's deep-voiced lover rumbled. Regales appeared out of nowhere—which was impressive because he was a really big guy—and wrapped one arm around his waist, tugging Theo's back to Regales's chest. "That's a private matter between mates."

Theo scoffed. "Sure, it is." He frowned. "You've wanted your mate for years, Dane. What's the hold-up?"

Huh. I'm kinda wondering the same thing.

Dane swallowed hard, as if he didn't know how to answer the other man's question.

Oh, wait.

"This is more sex talk, huh?" Danny whispered, his face heating. Grimacing, he focused on Theo. "I'm a virgin, and I think Dane's worried about hurting me." He held up his right arm. "Especially with this."

"Especially with that is one of the reasons Dane should be getting his ass in gear," Theo countered, shaking his head. "You'll heal like . . . three to four times faster after you bond."

"Wait." Danny glanced around the small group. "I will?"

Regales and Del both glared at Dane.

"You didn't tell him that?" Del demanded gruffly. "You didn't share the perks of humans mating with us?"

Dane actually seemed to wilt under the other pairs' stares. "I didn't want that to be his reason for choosing me." Dane almost whispered the words.

Danny never would have thought that Dane could be insecure in their . . . relationship. The man had always seemed so confident, so sure of himself. He always seemed to know the right things to say and do, making Danny feel special in countless ways.

Ignoring the way the others were exchanging glances, Danny turned in Dane's arms and faced him. He rested his left hand flat on his chest and rubbed his palm over his shifter's thick pectoral. Then Danny slid it up to cradle Dane's neck, encouraging him to dip his head a little.

"I already chose you, Dane," Danny murmured, enjoying the way Dane rested his forehead against Danny's, as if they were the only two people in existence. "I moved halfway across the country for you after only a few days."

"That's why I've been worried," Dane admitted softly. "Humans need to be wooed. They take longer to make decisions. I didn't want to pressure you."

Danny smiled at his silly shifter. "I sleep in your bed every night cuddled into your side," he pointed out. "We wake up and share some fun every morning. I've unpacked all my boxes." Shrugging, Danny knew he had to get Dane to understand. "I've never been in a relationship before, so I don't know if there's a specified length of time to consider it serious, but if you need me to ask you to marry me in order for you to realize I don't want to go anywhere, I will."

Dane sucked in a noisy breath, his eyes going wide. "You'd marry me?"

Snickering, Danny reminded him, "Well, Dakota did already say we were engaged." With a wink, he added, "That's the next step, isn't it?"

"Yeah." Dane grinned broadly at him. "Yeah, I guess it is."

"Well, then . . ." Danny couldn't believe what he was suggesting, but for some reason, it just felt right. "Or do I need to get you a ring first?"

Dane laughed. "No, I don't need a ring. Couldn't wear it when I shift anyway."

"Huh." Danny cocked his head. "That's another good point. I haven't actually seen your komodo dragon, yet, either."

"Well, that's not something I can really do in my backyard," Dane pointed out. "But if you want to see him, we can go somewhere secluded."

Danny grinned and nodded. "Let's put it on the list."

"Along with sightseeing," Miggs jumped in with a laugh. "I'd love to go on a paddleboat tour." His eyes lit up, showcasing his excitement. "Oh, and one of those ghost tour thingies. They'd be fun, right?"

Laughing, Danny nodded. "Sounds great."

"You know," Dakota cut in, announcing his presence. "Here ya go, man." He handed Danny an open bottle of lemonade. "I bet we could rent a paddleboat for you to have your wedding on." Then Dakota took a long swig of his beer.

Dane chuckled as he shook his head. "I don't know if I wanna go that far, but the tour would be nice."

Dakota shrugged. "So, when is this wedding gonna happen? We'll need to have a bachelor party." Waggling his brows, he added, "We could get some male strippers."

Wrinkling his nose, Danny admitted, "I'm not really into that. Sorry."

"Damn," Dakota grumbled. "All you mated dudes, spoiling my fun."

The group laughed before offering advice on not only wedding venues, but the best tourist places to check out in Savannah.

Walking into the house with Dane, Danny suddenly felt a healthy dose of nerves. Joking about being claimed while around the guys was one thing. Being a virgin, he knew actually doing it was something else.

When Danny reached the bedroom, he turned to find Dane standing in the doorway. His lover eyed him, worrying his lip. He stared at him with narrowed eyes and a tense furrow to his brows.

"Dane?" Danny asked tentatively.

Dane licked his lips once before offering, "If you're not ready, we don't have to do this." His voice came out soft, low, and filled with concern. "Just because the guys expect it—" Dane shook his head once. "What we've been doing is perfectly fine."

Danny wondered at his offer for a few seconds. Then it hit him. He realized Dane must have scented his nerves, so he was giving him an out.

Except, Danny had seen the lust and need in Dane's eyes while still at the party. It had matched his own every time Dane had nuzzled his temple or kissed his neck. Dane had told him that shifters have a heightened sense of smell. Danny had noticed the knowing smirks on some of the guys' faces as they'd interacted, so he figured they'd noticed their arousal, not that anyone ever said anything. According to Dane, if it wasn't family giving each other shit, it just wasn't done.

For that, Danny was appreciative.

Except, Danny really did want to be claimed. He wanted everything with his sexy shifter, especially that orgasmic bite Dane had told him about.

Danny just needed to figure out how to get it.

Ask for it.

There was a novel idea.

But how to?

Seeing how Dane held himself back, as if worried he would attack Danny if he drew too close, Danny decided to urge him nearer.

Danny lifted his casted arm and asked, "Will you help me with my shirt, please?"

Dane immediately lunged forward. "Of course, my mate." He gently gripped the hem of the polo shirt and eased it over Danny's head. Danny easily tugged out of one sleeve, then watched as Dane carefully pulled it off his injured wrist.

"Oh, I love these pearl snap shirts," Danny claimed, rubbing his and over Dane's top. It was true, too. He'd noticed at the barbeque how it was silky smooth to the touch. *Plus*—as he hooked the fingers of his left hand between snaps, Danny grinned and yanked. Laughing at Dane's shocked expression, Danny tore open every snap, revealing his shifter's expansive torso. "So easy to get off."

Then Danny rubbed his palm all over Dane's chest, enjoying the smooth flesh under his fingers as he explored each delineated muscle of his pectorals and abdominals. He even paused to rub his thumbs over his nipples. Upon hearing Dane's low growl, Danny peered at his lover from beneath his lashes.

"Yes?" Danny teased, going for sultry, although he had no idea if he pulled it off.

"Danny," Dane rumbled, his voice no more than a throaty

growl. "What are you doing?"

Shrugging, Danny admitted, "I'm trying to figure out how to turn you on, so you'll claim me."

Dane let out a low moan. His hands landed on Danny's hips, and he found himself rotated in the air. Ever-so-gently, Dane laid him in the middle of the bed. His lover proceeded to remove his shoes, socks, and pants.

When Dane revealed what was underneath, a whimper escaped him, and Danny felt ten feet tall. He'd been embarrassed as hell to go into the lingerie shop with Miggs, but the little shifter had convinced him. When he'd bought a few pairs of lacey boy shorts for himself, he didn't think his face would ever stop glowing.

Seeing the lust and approval in Dane's eyes made all the discomfort worth it.

"Oh, Danny," Dane purred, rubbing his hands up Danny's thighs. He rested his hand on either side of his groin, using his thumbs to pull the lacy fabric taut over his erection. "So, so, so pretty. Pretty, pretty."

Dane's deep brown eyes appeared to have darkened to black liquid pools of lust. His breathing came in ragged pants. Even sweat broke out on his forehead.

When Dane lifted his face to Danny's, he got the distinct impression that he was being stared at by both man and beast. A shiver of need worked through him at that feral expression, and his balls ached. His erection even twitched as a bead of pre-cum oozed from him.

Moaning, Dane pressed his nose to Danny's groin. "Gods, my mate," he stated on a moan. As he mouthed Danny's dick through his panties, Dane mumbled against his flesh. "I want you so badly, but I'm so close to the edge." Dane's eyes turned pleading even as he admitted, "I . . . I'm not sure I can be patient with you right now."

Danny reveled in the knowledge that he'd driven his big

controlled shifter to the edge. Spreading his legs wider, he offered himself.

"I don't want patient," Danny whispered. "I want you right now."

With a groan, Dane began to move, seeming to take him at his word. His hands and mouth moved everywhere, brushing, stroking, and teasing. Danny's body went up in flames.

CHAPTER ELEVEN

Dane knew he'd waited too long. He'd so desperately wanted to give Danny time to choose him, to accept everything. He just hadn't anticipated how the feel of holding his delectable little human in his arms every night would feel.

His animal rode him hard to dominate, to possess and claim. Even though Dane was on the same page, he knew his sweet human was a virgin — never been touched. He couldn't just plow in and rut away.

That didn't mean he had to take things too slowly, though. Not that he ever planned to discuss it with Danny, but he had over a century and a half of experience. He knew how to play a body.

Reining in his dominant need, Dane began laying brushing touches, licks, nips, kisses, and suckles to every inch of Danny's luscious body he could reach. At the same time, he reached over and dug the lube out of his nightstand drawer. After dropping that on the bed, he shifted his hand into his komodo's claws.

Not every shifter had the ability to change a certain body part, but he and his brothers could. Del had taught them. They didn't need to do it often in their line of work, but they practiced it together, in private, keeping those who knew of his abilities to a small few.

Using his lethal claws, Dane shredded his jeans. He couldn't bear to pull himself away long enough to even undress. After Dane had kicked off his shoes, his socks ended up in ribbons on the floor, too.

Blissfully naked, Dane returned his claws to hands and continued stroking every inch of his mate's skin. He returned his mouth to Danny's erection, mouthing and sucking it through the thin, sexy material. The pretty blue swirls of lace did nothing to hide his human's unique scent, the sweet flavor of his pre-cum.

Ambrosia.

The nectar of the gods.

Dane grabbed the lube and, as he sucked his mate's cock head through his panties, poured a healthy dollop onto his fingers. Then he returned to petting, scraping, and teasing his lover's toned flesh. At the same time, Dane used a thumb to push aside the scrap of material hiding his star from his fingers and began massaging that opening he desperately needed inside.

To Dane's pleasure, Danny's body easily accepted his first finger. He had to guess his little mate had played with himself before, but that was a conversation for another time. After working his slick finger in and out of him a couple of times, Dane pushed a second digit deep inside of him.

Feeling the tension and pressure encasing him, Dane levered up higher. He sucked one of Danny's nipples into his mouth, stimulating the bud. That did the trick.

Danny's chute relaxed as he arched into Dane's touch. He heard his mate cry out as he pushed his chest against his mouth. Flicking his tongue against Danny's hardened nipple, Dane twisted his fingers, searching.

Hearing Danny's scream, Dane quickly transferred his mouth back to his lace-covered cock head. He sucked his mate's cream through the fabric, enjoying his human's deliciousness. Taking advantage of Danny's pleasure, Dane slipped a third finger into his body, working him open some more.

Dane peered up Danny's body, gauging his readiness with

more than just the feel of his inner chute muscles. His human's chest rose and fell in slow breaths. His hips wriggled just a little. Even his lips were parted and cheeks flushed as he whimpered. His need continued to perfume the air.

Perfect.

Easing his fingers free of Danny's channel, Dane quickly grabbed a pair of pillows, piling them on top of each other. Then he gripped his lover, laying his chest on them. "No pressure on your arm," Dane ordered, urging Danny to slide it forward. "Relax on the pillows."

"Yeah," Danny panted. "Okay."

Grabbing the lube again, Dane turned his attention to Danny's gorgeous, pert derriere. He moaned upon seeing the full mounds showcased by the lacy blue fabric. As tempting as it was to tear them off, Dane couldn't resist leaving them.

All it would take was to push them aside a smidge, and Dane could fuck his mate with them on.

Oh, yeah.

Dane couldn't resist.

After slathering his dick with more lube than he could ever remember using, Dane did just that. He palmed his mate's left butt cheek and pulled it to the side. With his right hand, Dane slid his crown around the fabric, revealing his lubed and stretched opening.

Touching his swollen crown to Danny's hole, Dane felt a shudder work through him.

Now, now, now.

Dane could practically feel his beast chanting in the back of his mind.

With his last shred of control, Dane draped over Danny's back. He pressed forward just a smidge, making the hole he wanted to enter flex. Another tremble worked through him, and he moaned in Danny's ear.

"Please, my mate," Dane begged. "Tell me I can have you."

"Yes," Danny replied on a pant. "Yes, god, now."

Unable to fight both his nature and his mate's plea, Dane did as requested. He thrust. Even after his bulbous head popped inside his human's body, he couldn't stop. Dane continued to push, to sink deeper and deeper into the love of his life.

Sweet, exquisite pressure soon encased every inch of his length, forcing Dane to stop. A shudder rippled through him. Every instinct within him told him to ease back and do it again.

Only the tight squeeze holding him damn near in a death-grip stayed his action.

Panting harshly, Dane struggled to keep still. He knew he needed to give his beautiful human time to adjust. As a large shifter, he wasn't a small man, and he'd just plowed his way in, burrowing deep.

He should —

"Please move," Danny whined, wriggling beneath him. "God, you feel — oh, god, move."

"Yesssss," Dane snarled, and he did just that.

Dane couldn't help himself. He started up a swift rhythm, pulling back and thrusting back inside. The hot squeeze along the nerve endings of his throbbing shaft went straight to his balls. His testicles tightened, and he gritted his teeth, fearing he would come before pleasing his mate.

Levering up a bit, Dane forced his rutting body to adjust his angle.

Danny cried out and arched beneath him.

Relief flooding him, Dane knew he'd found it — his mate's prostate. He continued to peg Danny's gland, sweat dripping from his temples as he tightened his gut with determination. Dane would send his mate flying before — then Danny was there.

His sweet love screamed his pleasure to the ceiling, arching and jolting beneath him. The sound was music to his ears, and he buried himself deep. His balls pulled tight, and he stopped fighting it.

As Dane's orgasm rolled over him, his dragon's fangs lengthened. Leaning close, he licked over Danny's skin where his neck met his shoulder. Unable to resist the siren call to bond, Dane sank his fangs deep into his mate's succulent flesh.

Danny tensed beneath him. A second later, as his blood flowed across Dane's tongue and he couldn't resist sucking for more, his mate groaned and jolted beneath him. Dane's mouth filled with Danny's life-fluid, the heady goodness lighting up his taste buds. At the same time, the exquisite aroma of Danny's seed flooded the room with a fresh dose, telling Dane that his gorgeous human had come once more.

After drinking a couple more mouthfuls, Dane eased his dragon's long fangs from Danny's shoulder. He lapped over the marks, licking up the blood as he sealed them. His komodo dragon rumbled with happiness in his mind as they both admired the deep, deep claiming scar they'd left in Danny's flesh.

Gorgeous . . . and all mine.

At last.

Dane nuzzled Danny's neck, his temple, then pressed a few kisses over his mark and the man's nape. Hearing his mate sigh, feeling his shivers against his body, he smiled with pleasure. Dane loved that even after getting his mate off three times, he could still affect him so.

Carefully, Dane eased his half-hard prick from Danny's pliant body. He heard his man's quiet moan, and knew from experience, a lover's retreat could be an odd sensation. Reaching down, encountering silk, reminded him of Danny's beautiful undies.

Such a special mate.

Even as Dane thought that, he slid his finger under the beautiful fabric and massaged his lover's opening. The feel of his seed oozing from Danny's body only caused his pride to swell even further. His cock even gave a half-hearted twitch as if readying for another round.

"Relax," Dane crooned before licking his ear, enjoying the taste of the sweat on his flesh. "Just helping you relax. I know the emptiness can feel weird at first."

Danny hummed as he turned his head. He looked at him lazily. "Not totally empty," he said with a snicker. His smile turned loopy. "Wow. Can't wait to do that again."

Dane chuckled before pecking a kiss to the corner of his lover's mouth. "I'll be right back to clean you up."

After humming again, Danny relaxed, and Dane eased off the bed and hurried to the bathroom.

By the time Dane returned, his sexy mate had fallen asleep. Even when he rolled his human over, pulled the now-cum-sopping boy shorts from his body, and cleaned him up, his lover remained comatose.

Grinning with smug pleasure, Dane pulled the blankets over Danny before climbing in and curling his arms around the love of his life.

Following up with Miggs's ideas, Dane joined with him and his brothers to check out a few scenic sightseeing areas.

They enjoyed a land and sea combo tour, which included a trolley tour followed by a riverboat cruise. Dakota insisted on a culinary and culture walking food tour, because what self-respecting shifter wouldn't jump at the chance of checking out different foods. To Dane's surprise, Del had found the haunted pub walk tour in Savannah's historic district fascinating. Del had even texted Dane about trying some of the other haunted tours.

My eldest brother finds the idea of spirits fascinating. Who knew?

"So, when do you expect to be ready to go back to work, Enforcer Dane?"

Dane focused on Head Enforcer Mycroft. The dominant cheetah shifter arched one brow while relaxing back in his seat. Grinning, Dane shook his head while he shrugged.

"I'm cleared for another two weeks of leave, and I intend to use it," Dane told the head council enforcer. "It's been years since I've taken a vacation, and I'm getting everything together for my marriage."

Mycroft barked a laugh, a smile twitching his usually stoic features. "I'd heard a few rumors that you planned to get married. I wasn't totally certain they were true, though." He leaned forward, threading his fingers before him. "Well, make sure I get an invitation."

Rising from his seat, Dane nodded. "That I will, sir."

Chuckling, Mycroft waved him away, and Dane knew he was free to go. He'd stopped into Shifter Council Headquarters to answer a few questions. The answers had been needed to tie up loose ends on a mission he'd been on nearly six months before.

Sometimes, paperwork sucked.

Okay. Paperwork always sucks.

Dane grinned happily as he headed out of the building. He wouldn't have to worry about anything for another couple of weeks. Well, not about that anyway.

Instead, Dane wanted to buy his gorgeous human the perfect ring. Just because Dane couldn't wear one didn't mean Danny couldn't. With that thought in mind, he rode his *Harley* into town.

Trundling along the streets, Dane searched for the shop he wanted. He was in old town, where most of the shops were still owned by locals. Whenever possible, he always liked to patron local small businesses. In this case, that worked in his favor, because Dane remembered a store he'd always wanted to check out.

A jewelry shop that made custom pieces.

Dane parked as close to the store as possible. After locking up his helmet and jacket, he threaded his fingers through his hair. He scratched his scalp a bit before lowering his arms and jogging across the street, avoiding the trolley in the process.

Entering the store, Dane stopped inside a few steps. There were several glass display cases as well as shelves holding carousels of necklaces, rings, and other jewelry. Mirrors were hung in strategic locations so one could try something on and see how it looked.

"Good afternoon, sir," a pleasant-looking older man greeted, coming from a door in the back. "Can I help you find anything today?"

Dane dipped his head in a quick nod. "I'm looking for a wedding band." Because he didn't want there to be any mis-understandings, he quickly added, "Something I can give to my future husband."

The man didn't miss a step as he nodded. "Of course." He beckoned off to the left. "What's your young man's taste?" he inquired. "Gold, silver, platinum, gems?" He began pointing at different obviously masculine rings. "Something with a thick band or something more delicate?"

"Wow." For a moment, the selection blew Dane's mind. He roved over the offerings. "So many possibilities."

Chuckling softly, the aging human dipped his head in a nod. "Well, that's life now-a-days." He smiled, the corners of his eyes crinkling. "With acceptance comes options." Resting his wrinkled hand on the counter, he urged, "So, tell me about your man."

Dane sighed, a smile curving his lips as he thought about Danny. "He's ... everything I could possibly want and more."

The old man tipped his head back a little and laughed. "Ah, spoken like a man truly in love." Reaching across the glass counter, he patted Dane's arm. "I'm happy for you." He straightened, urging, "Tell me more. Size? Shape? Have you noticed him wearing jewelry in the past?"

Shaking his head slowly, Dane began, "No, on the jewelry, and he likes to work with his hands." He narrowed his eyes as he thought some more. "He's average height, fine-boned, a little slender." Unable to help himself, Dane mumbled, "Fits in my arms perfectly."

Grinning broadly, the old man nodded. "Well, perhaps one of these platinum bands might be more to his liking. They can be as wide or slender as you wish." He pointed to a tray with a variety of rings. "They can take quite a beating without getting a scratch, dent, or nick."

Dane hummed, focusing on them. He was about to lean toward one when he spotted a completely different set of trays—ones with non-traditional gems held in a display of twisted platinum that created animal shapes. Unable to help himself, Dane pointed.

"I'd like to see that one, please."

While surprised, the old man obeyed. "Can't say these are wedding rings."

"My guy's not traditional," Dane mumbled as he took the item that had caught his eye. "And neither am I." As he took in the amber stone—reminiscent of his mate's hazel eyes—as well and the setting that appeared almost dragon-like, Dane grinned. "This is perfect."

"Really?"

Chuckling, Dane nodded. "Can you size that?"

"Of course. It'll take a few days."

"Not a problem." Now that Dane had made a choice, one that he loved, the tension in his shoulders eased. "I'll take it."

Dane didn't mind that the old man eyed him curiously. He paid and, with a spring in his step, headed back toward his bike.

He didn't make it.

Crossing an alley, a man stepped up beside him and

pressed the barrel of a gun into his side. "Turn left," he ordered coldly. "Someone wants to talk to you."

Dane obeyed even as he searched for a way to twist and get the gun from his back. As soon as he rounded a corner, the man shot him. Even as Dane realized it was a tranquilizer gun and lunged for the guy, the guy hopped out of the way.

The dart took effect, and Dane fell.

CHAPTER TWELVE

Danny hummed as he scrubbed the dishes one-handed — sort of. He had a giant kitchen glove on his right one, allowing him to use his cast while washing. Using the tips of his fingers wasn't easy, but he managed.

Less than a week after being claimed, Danny could already feel a difference in his wrist. While he was damn grateful that his accelerated healing was already kicking in — no one wanted to be in pain unnecessarily — he knew that wasn't why he'd pushed Dane to bond with him. He'd wanted forever with his shifter.

Now, if I can just convince my mate that I'm not going to freak out if I see his animal form.

Danny knew why Dane was leery to shift in front of him. He hadn't reacted well to Dakota — not at all. In his defense, however, that had been the same day they'd tried to explain and in the confines of a hotel room with people he hardly knew.

There has to be a way.

Finishing the dishes, Danny wondered who could help him convince his mate. Dane had mentioned going somewhere private. Maybe if he convinced his brothers to meet wherever they normally shifted, Dane would be more willing.

As Danny finished drying his hands, Dane's cell phone began to ring. His shifter had left it with him, since Danny didn't have one. Picking up a new phone was still on their *to do* list.

Smiling, Danny headed over to the device, his thoughts

consumed with the activities they'd been engaging in that always distracted them from going anywhere. Lots and lots of mind-blowing sex, which Danny totally enjoyed. Only the fact that Dane had to meet with someone at Council Headquarters was why Danny had been left home alone.

Seeing Del's name on Dane's phone as he picked it up, Danny answered, growing excited. He could ask the man immediately. Before Danny could say a word, Del spoke.

"Your mate's father is on the move. He's headed our way. Are you with him?"

Danny felt his breath catch in his chest. He opened and closed his mouth.

"Dane?" Del barked.

"M-My father's coming here?" Danny squeaked, finally finding his voice. "Why?"

"Danny?" Del's voice filled with confusion. "What are you doing with Dane's phone? Is he there?"

Swallowing hard, Danny replied, "Dane went to Council Headquarters for a meeting with someone named Mycroft. We haven't gotten around to getting me a new phone, yet, so he left his with me." Unable to help himself, he demanded, "What's going on with my father?"

Del let out a low growly noise. "Your father is unstable. I'm sure you realized that when you were picking up your shit."

Danny winced even as he mumbled, "Yeah."

"Well, I don't know what his end game is, but his credit cards say he's headed this way," Del told him. Danny remained quiet because he had no idea what to say, and Del kept talking. "From what Theo's told me, he's up to his ears in credit card debt, and his bank account's in the red. A man like that is desperate, so you sit tight and wait for Dane to come home. You got me?"

"Yes," Danny forced himself to reply, although his voice was anything but steady.

Growling, Del repeated, "You stay there. I'll call Mycroft, who can update Dane." After a second of hesitation, the man added, "I'm sure Dane will be back in no time."

"Um, thank you for the heads-up," Danny stated, since he didn't know what else to say.

Del grunted something that could have been *you're welcome*, but Danny wasn't certain. Then the line went dead.

Sighing, Danny stared at the phone. He carefully settled on the edge of the sofa and focused on his breathing for a few minutes. Then he stared at the phone again.

His father was on his way. For all he knew, he was already in the area. Danny knew what he wanted. It was always the same.

Money.

Dialing a number Danny's mother had forced him to memorize when he was five years old, he called his father's cell phone.

It rang once, twice, three times . . . then—"Who is this?"

"Hello, Father." Danny tried to make his voice come out strong, sure, and confident. Sadly, he was pretty sure he'd failed miserably. Still, he persevered. "Why are you coming south?"

"Daniel." Only Danny's father could make his given name sound like a curse. His laugh was cold and heartless. "Don't know what you heard, but I'm already here."

"What do you want?"

As if I don't already know.

"You," his father declared.

Okay, that's a surprise.

"What? Why? You hate me."

"You're mine, boy!" his father roared. "No damn biker is gonna take you and your paycheck away from me." His voice took on a fanatical quality. "I paid for your shit for years, and now you owe me."

Unable to help himself, Danny muttered, "I thought you

didn't want a faggot living in your house."

"See, that's the other little problem. Can't have you mar-ryin' your damn biker and draggin' our family name through the sludge." Danny's father's voice turned hard and snarly. "Saw your announcement in the paper. Came here to stop it."

Danny opened his mouth to question his comment, then snapped it shut just as quickly.

Right. Dakota said he was going to place an announcement. Shit!

"And lucky me, my guys found your guy walkin' down the street." His father's laugh was just as cruel as he remem-bered. "He's here, unconscious but alive." That claim caused Danny's heart to threaten to stop. "So, here's what you're gonna do," his father continued. "You're gonna meet me at this warehouse. Just you. I'll let your fucking faggot biker go, and we'll go home." With a snicker, his father finished, "You'll continue giving me your money, and I won't pay my associates to kill your faggot biker."

Oh shit. Shit, shit, shit.

Dane and Dakota had warned Danny that something was off about his father, but he hadn't paid attention. Out of re-spect for his mother and the past, he hadn't wanted his father hurt. Danny had just wanted to move on.

And now, that request is going to bite me in the ass.

Forcing his voice to come out even, Danny asked, "Where do you want me to meet you?" After he'd written down the address, he mumbled, "I don't have a car, so it'll take me about twenty minutes to be there."

"Hurry up," his father demanded before disconnecting the call.

Danny would do anything for his Dane, including walking into danger . . . but he wasn't stupid.

As quick as could be, he texted Del a message with the ad-dress. Ignoring the man's return call, he instead called an *Uber*.

"Well, my goober faggot of a son bought it."

Dane recognized Danny's father's sniveling voice. The drug had only knocked him halfway out, his animal and his genetics easily burning it from his system. Instead, Dane had chosen to stay still and quiet so he could learn who these fuckers with Danny's father were.

"Good. Your son's looks are perfect for several of our clients," the blond male who'd held a gun on him and shot him stated. A low chuckle entered his voice. "We'll have a bidding war for sure." His cold thin lips were curved into a smile as he patted Danny's father on the shoulder. "Once we have your son, all your debts will be paid."

"Thanks." Glancing around the warehouse, Mister Nunez asked, "Hey, any of you got a beer or some whiskey or something? I wanna drink."

With his eyelids cracked, Dane watched the blond man snort as he waved at a black-haired guy. That man pulled a small flask from inside his jacket, which he handed to Danny's father. The man took a deep swig followed by a second.

It took everything Dane had in him to stay still as he watched Danny's father begin to choke, followed by coughing, then ending in falling to his knees as he hacked and gagged. His face turned red, then purple. Spittle dripped down his chin as the man dropped to the floor. In seconds, the distinctive scent of death reached Dane's sensitive nostrils.

"Gods, what a moron," the black-haired guy grumbled. "Drunks." He rolled his eyes. "Such assholes."

The blond shrugged a shoulder, casting a dismissive glance Danny's father's way. "Eh, they have their uses. He's given us what we need. A twinky, pale, hazel-eyed boy." Glancing at his watch, he added, "Get ready to dose him. We need to be out of here in five after he arrives."

"What about this guy?" The third man was a huge brunette with a gruff voice that sounded as if he gargled glass every morning. "Want me to kill him?"

The blond laughed. "Naw. Everyone is worth a few bucks. Even a big bastard like him. Throw him in the back when the car arrives."

"Got it."

Dane decided he'd heard enough. As soon as the huge brunette drew close enough, he lunged to his feet. Grabbing the guy, he used his shifter strength and tossed him the length of the warehouse.

"What the hell!" the black-haired guy cried even as the blond pulled the gun.

Having heard these men's depravity—selling people and threatening his mate—Dane had no qualms about shifting. His change happened in seconds, and the dart the blond tried to hit him with bounced off his thick hide. He swung his tail and smacked the man, sending him skidding across the cement floor. When the guy slammed into the wall and lay still, Dane did hope he lived, only because he knew Del could extract information out of him.

Swinging his head around, Dane snapped his jaws, closing them over the asshole slaver's torso. His teeth sank deep. As soon as he was certain his life force would ebb, he yanked his teeth free and flung the human.

"Dane?"

Spinning, Dane faced the speaker. He spotted Danny in the doorway and froze. For several long seconds, they just stared at each other.

Then Dane rumbled low in his throat as he took several steps forward.

Danny whispered, "God, that is you isn't it, Dane?" His gaze remained focused on him as he started toward him slowly. "A-Are you okay? Can I—Can I touch you?" His hands were lifted in a non-combative move, and he swept his focus over his massive frame.

Rumbling quietly, Dane took a few more steps forward before lowering his head and stretching toward Danny as long as his head would reach.

"Wow." Danny rested his hands on Dane's head, stroking softly. "Just . . . amazing."

For several long minutes, Dane reveled in the feel of his mate petting his hide. He'd never had anyone do that before—never had wanted anyone to. His mate's hands, however, they felt beyond amazing.

"Well, fuck, bro." Dakota's voice broke into his moment. "What the hell happened in here?"

"You need to shift," Del cut in. "I have clothes."

Of course he does.

Del always came prepared.

After nuzzling Danny's chest one more time, Dane shifted. As soon as he reached his human form, he grabbed his mate and pulled him against his chest. "I'm so sorry," Dane whispered. "There wasn't anything I could do."

Danny lifted his chin and frowned at Dane. "What are you talking about?"

"Your father." Dane peered in the dead man's direction. "They gave him a flask of liquor. It must have been laced with poison." Shaking his head, he muttered, "He was dead in seconds."

Rubbing Dane's jaw with his good hand, Danny whispered, "I understand. Not your fault." He lifted on his tiptoes and pecked his jaw. "After talking to him, I understand that he was nothing but a threat to us. I know this sounds weird but . . ." He blew out a breath. "I just appreciate that his blood isn't on your hands even though he's out of the way."

Dane sighed with relief as he took his mate's lips in a fierce kiss.

Too bad Del had to interrupt. "Get dressed," he ordered,

handing Dane a set of clothes. "What about these other guys."

"We need to take those who are alive with us, even though they're human," Dane admitted. "They're part of a human trafficking ring."

Del snarled. "Got it."

Dane knew his brother would take care of things, so after he yanked on the clothes, he wrapped his arm around Danny's waist and began guiding him out of the warehouse.

"Hey!"

Turning, Dane caught the keys Dakota tossed his way, realizing they were to his *Harley*.

"Off to the right."

"Thanks, bro!" Dane called back with a grin.

Then Dane focused on Danny. "You ready to go home?"

Danny pressed against him. "More than." Staring at him in concern, he asked, "Are you sure you're all right?"

After a kiss to his sweet mate's upturned lips, Dane assured, "Absolutely." He barked a laugh. "They weren't expecting a shifter, so I just had to bide my time." With a wink, Dane turned his mate in the direction Dakota had indicated. "Let's go home." With a wink, he added, "We have a wedding to plan."

Beyond happy with the way Danny snuggled into his side, Dane left those problems to his brother and headed home for some snuggles with his mate.

ABOUT THE AUTHOR

Charlie started writing fantasy when she was eight, and after stumbling onto her first erotic romance at age nineteen, she realized her true calling. She now focuses on writing gay erotic romance, normally of the paranormal variety, with heroes of all kinds. With the help and support of her husband, Charlie finally fulfilled one of her life-long goals . . . move to acreage with her horses. You can often find her curled up with her laptop and a cup of tea or glass of wine, creating her next adventure. Charlie enjoys exploring the mountains of her new Oregon home on horseback, 4-wheeler, or motorcycle.

She can be reached at ch.richards2010@yahoo.com
Or visit her at www.charlie-richards.com.